Light blue ... **open when before they'd been closed**

Her lips parted on a shocked gasp. Then a scream burning in her throat, she tried to utter it, but a big palm clamped tight over her mouth. His skin was rough and warm against her lips.

The man sat up, the body bag falling off his wide shoulders to pool at his lean waist, leaving his muscled chest bare but for a light dusting of golden hair and a bloodied bandage over his ribs.

Macy twisted her neck and her wrist, trying to wrestle free of his grasp. But he held on tightly, the pressure just short of being painful. Her heart pounded out a crazy rhythm as fear coursed through her veins.

She had to break loose of him and run out the open door. With his lower body still zipped in the bag, he wouldn't be able to chase her, and maybe the elevator would be back. Or she'd take the stairs…

"You're safe," he murmured, his voice a deep rumble in that heavily muscled chest as he assured her, "I'm not going to hurt you."

LISA CHILDS

LAWMAN LOVER

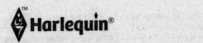

TORONTO NEW YORK LONDON
AMSTERDAM PARIS SYDNEY HAMBURG
STOCKHOLM ATHENS TOKYO MILAN MADRID
PRAGUE WARSAW BUDAPEST AUCKLAND

To Kimberly Duffy, for always being there for me.
Your friendship means the world to me!

Recycling programs
for this product may
not exist in your area.

ISBN-13: 978-0-373-69605-5

LAWMAN LOVER

Copyright © 2012 by Lisa Childs-Theeuwes

www.Harlequin.com

Printed in U.S.A.

ABOUT THE AUTHOR

Bestselling, award-winning author Lisa Childs writes paranormal and contemporary romance for Harlequin Books. She lives on thirty acres in west Michigan with her husband, two daughters, a talkative Siamese and a long-haired Chihuahua who thinks she's a Rottweiler. Lisa loves hearing from readers, who can contact her through her website, www.lisachilds.com, or snail mail address, P.O. Box 139, Marne, MI 49435.

Books by Lisa Childs

HARLEQUIN INTRIGUE

*Outlaws

All backlist available in ebook. Don't miss any of our special offers. Write to us at the following address for information on our newest releases.

Harlequin Reader Service
U.S.: 3010 Walden Ave., P.O. Box 1325, Buffalo, NY 14269
Canadian: P.O. Box 609, Fort Erie, Ont. L2A 5X3

CAST OF CHARACTERS

Rowe Cusack—His cover blown, the DEA agent finds the only way out of Blackwoods Penitentiary is in a body bag.

Macy Kleyn—She gave up everything to help her brother out of prison, but helping Rowe Cusack may cost her more—her life and her heart.

Warden James—The corrupt prison official will do anything—and kill anyone—to protect his illegal operations.

Jedidiah Kleyn—The convict put his sister in jeopardy with only the promise from a targeted DEA agent that he'd protect her.

Sheriff Griffin York—Can the lawman be trusted or is he working for the man who made significant contributions to his recent campaign?

Dr. Bernard—The Blackwoods county coroner may know where all the warden's bodies are buried and may even be willing to help him bury a few more.

Special Agent Donald Jackson—Rowe's handler in the DEA may have been the one who gave up his real identity to the warden.

Elliot Sutherland—Macy's one good friend in Blackwoods might just want more.

DEA Special Agents Tillman, Hernandez and O'Neil—One of them finds the proof that Rowe is still alive and is determined that he and Macy don't remain that way.

Chapter One

The cell door slid open with the quick buzz of the disabled security alarm and the clang of heavy metal. Rowe Cusack swung his legs over the side of his bunk and jumped down onto the concrete floor. Had the warden reinstated his privileges?

Rowe couldn't understand why they'd been suspended in the first place. He hadn't started the fight in the cafeteria even though he had ended it. But the warden had punished him anyway and ignored Rowe's demands to use the phone.

He needed to make the call that would get him the hell out of...*hell*. His instincts tightened his guts into knots; he was pretty sure his cover had been blown.

But how? He had been going undercover for years before he had joined the Drug Enforcement Administration, and even as a rookie with the Detroit Police Department he had never been discovered.

"Hey, guard," Rowe called out, disrupting the eerie quiet of predawn in the cell block. "What's going on?"

Even if his privileges had been reinstated, they wouldn't allow him to make a call at this hour. He hadn't been allowed one in over a week. No visitors either, not even a letter or an email. After just a few days of no contact, his handler, in his guise as Rowe's attorney, should have checked in on him. Or Special Agent Jackson should have had him pulled out. Leaving him in here with no backup and no real weapon for self-protection, if his cover had been blown, was like leaving him for dead.

"You got a new roommate," a deep voice announced, and a hulking shadow darkened the cell. "Get out of here, Petey."

Rowe's scrawny cell mate scrambled out of the bottom bunk and flattened his back against the wall as he squeezed through the cell door opening around the giant of a man entering it.

Rowe reached for his homemade shiv, closing his fingers around the toothbrush handle. Even in the dim glow of the night security lights, he recognized the man whom he'd given a wide berth since his incarceration. His flimsy weapon wouldn't be much protection against the burly giant.

"What the hell do you want?" he asked the monster of a man.

"Same thing you do," the deep voice murmured. "To get the hell out of here."

"There's no escape route in here." Rowe had checked for one. He'd had some tough assignments over his six years with the DEA, but getting locked up like an animal, with animals, was his worst mission yet. From between his shoulder blades, sweat trickled down his back, and panic pressed on his chest.

Damn claustrophobia…

He'd fought it since he was a kid, refusing to let it

rule or limit his life. But maybe he should have used it as a reason to get out of taking this assignment.

"You're my escape route," Jedidiah Kleyn said, stepping closer. Light from the dim overhead bulb glinted off his bald head and his dark eyes. The eyes of a cold-blooded killer.

This was the last person Rowe would have wanted to learn his real identity. He shook his head in denial. "You got the wrong guy."

The prisoner laughed; the sharp, loud noise sounded like a hammer pounding nails into Rowe's casket. "That's not what I hear."

"What do you hear?" He wondered how the man heard anything; Rowe wasn't the only prisoner who gave him a wide berth. Nobody wanted to mess with this man, and so as to not risk pissing him off, nobody talked to him.

"I hear that you ask a lot of questions." Kleyn stepped even closer. Rowe was over six feet tall and muscular, but this guy was taller. Broader, like a brick wall of mean. "I hear that you stick your nose where it doesn't belong."

Rowe lifted his chin, refusing to retreat. Since he'd basically raised himself, he had learned young to never back down from a fight. He damn sure couldn't back down in here—not even if the fight killed him. "I've never bothered you."

Kleyn laughed again, like a swinging hammer. "Nobody does. They all know better."

"So do I," Rowe admitted. "I've heard stuff about you, too, even before I got transferred to Blackwoods to serve out the rest of my sentence." A few years ago

Jedidiah Kleyn's horrendous crimes had been all over the news. So even though Rowe's cover claimed he'd been incarcerated in another state penitentiary, he still would have heard about the killer.

Kleyn expelled a weary sigh, as if it bothered him to be the topic of discussion. "Well, you shouldn't believe everything you hear."

"No," Rowe agreed. "I didn't pay all that much attention to what anyone had to say about you."

"That's because I have nothing to do with drugs," Kleyn said. "And that seems to be all you want to know about."

Rowe's gut clenched. Damn. He had been careful, as he always was. In the three weeks he'd been locked up in the maximum-security prison, he'd done more listening than talking. And he had saved his questions, only asking a few and of people who'd seemed to think nothing of them. He'd learned years ago when and who to talk to so as to not raise any suspicions, and he hadn't had a problem before.

What the hell had gone so wrong this time? No one could have recognized him; before the Drug Enforcement Administration had sent him undercover, his handlers had checked the inmate roster to make sure Rowe had never had contact with any of them.

"Drugs have nothing to do with why I'm not that interested in the gossip about you," he said, trying to convince the other man. "I don't care what people say about you because I'm just not scared of you."

A grin slashed deep grooves in Kleyn's face. "And here you are, with more to fear from me than anyone else in this damn hellhole."

"Why's that?" he asked. Except for the crimes Kleyn had committed, Rowe had had no problem with him. A different inmate had attacked him in the cafeteria. The guy had been big, but Rowe had overpowered him without much effort. He worried he wouldn't be able to handle Kleyn as easily.

"You've heard about me," he said, "so you know why everybody leaves me alone."

Rowe nodded. Unfortunately he knew. If he hadn't had an assignment to complete, he might have sought out Kleyn, and discovered just how well he could handle a fight with the intimidating giant, in order to dole out a little physical justice for Kleyn's crimes. "You're a cop killer."

"And you're a cop."

His cover was definitely blown.

Rowe tightened his grip on the shiv. But could he bury the flimsy weapon deep enough to stop the big guy from killing him?

His throat burned as he forced a laugh. "That's crazy. Sure, I asked some questions. I saw what's going on in here, and I wanted in on the action. Getting busted for dealing is the reason I'm in here, man."

"You're in here to investigate Blackwoods Penitentiary and find out how far the corruption goes. Just a few guards or all the way to the top."

The short hair lifted on his nape as the prisoner relayed word for word the synopsis Rowe's handler had given him for his current assignment.

"You really should have asked me," Kleyn replied, "because I can definitely answer that question for you." He lifted his beefy hand, and light glinted off the long blade of the big weapon he carried. "All the way to the top."

Rowe stepped back but only to widen his stance and brace himself for what he suspected would be the battle of his life. For his life. "You don't want to do this."

"No," the man agreed with a sigh of resignation. "But I have to. Only one of us can come out of this cell alive."

Rowe intended to fight like hell to make sure he was the one to survive. Kleyn had already killed too many people. So, his flimsy weapon clasped tight in his hand, he lunged toward his would-be assassin.

MACY KLEYN'S FINGERS TREMBLED on the tab of the body bag. Her heart thudded slowly and heavily with dread. Could this be…? She drew in a deep breath of the cool air blowing through the vents in the morgue. Then she closed her eyes in fear of what she might see when she unzipped the bag.

"Macy, you got this?" a man called out to her from the hall. "Dr. Bernard won't be here for another hour or so. The sheriff and the warden called him back out to the prison. So I gotta bring the van out there again."

Why? The body, from that morning's fatal stabbing, was here, inside the black plastic bag lying across the gurney. She shivered, and not from the cold air, as she realized the only reason the county coroner had returned to the prison.

Someone else had died.

"Just shove him inside a drawer until Dr. Bernard gets here," Bob, the driver said, his voice growing fainter as he headed toward the elevator, which would carry him to the hospital floors above ground.

"Sure, I'll take care of him," she said, her words echoing off the floors and walls, which were all white tile but for the one wall of stainless steel doors. Her reflection bounced back from one of those doors—her dark hair pulled into a ponytail, leaving her face stark and pale, her dark eyes wide with fear. She had to stow the body behind one of those doors, inside a cold metal drawer.

But first she had to see if the nightmare she had been having for the past three years had come true. Had her brother—her dear, sweet, protective older brother— died in the awful, soul-sucking place that he never should have been?

Tears of frustration stung her eyes at the injustice of his conviction. He wasn't a killer. Not Jed. Now had he been killed, just like she saw him die in the nightmares from which she always awoke screaming?

Macy had given up so much to be close to him, to keep him going while they tried to find evidence for an appeal. But the whole time she tried to prove his innocence, she heard a clock ticking inside her head. Blackwoods Penitentiary was the worst possible place her brother could have been sentenced. Prisoners were more likely to leave the facility in body bags than to be paroled. Not that her brother had any chance for parole; he had been sentenced to life without possibility of parole for each of the murders he'd been convicted of committing. Two life sentences.

Had they both just been commuted?

She drew in another deep breath, bracing herself for

what she might find. Then she tightened her grip on the zipper tab and tugged it down to reveal the stabbing victim from that morning.

Blond hair fell across his forehead, thick lashes lay against sharp cheekbones, and his sculpted lips pressed tight together. It wasn't Jed.

Macy's breath caught then shuddered out; her relief tempered with guilt and regret. Whoever this man was—he was too young to die, probably only in his early thirties. And, not that it mattered, he was ridiculously handsome. He was also a convict, though, and unlikely to have been innocent like Jed. She hated to think of anyone else being so unjustly accused and sentenced…to death at Blackwoods.

She reached for the zipper again but as she lifted the tab, a hand closed over hers. Her breath catching in her throat, she jerked her attention back to the body. Light blue eyes stared up at her, open now where just moments before they had been closed.

Her lips parted on a shocked gasp, with a scream burning in her throat. But she couldn't utter that scream. A big palm clamped tight over her mouth. Instead of being cold and clammy, his skin was rough and warm against her lips. This was no corpse but a living and breathing man.

He sat up, the body bag falling off his wide shoulders to settle at his lean waist, leaving his muscled chest bare but for a light dusting of golden hair and a bloodied bandage over his ribs.

Macy twisted her neck and her wrist, trying to wrestle free of his grasp. But he held on tightly, the pressure just short of being painful. Her heart pounded out a crazy rhythm as fear coursed through her veins.

She had to break loose and run out the open door. With his lower body still zipped in the bag, he wouldn't be able to chase her, and maybe the elevator would be back. Or she would take the stairs…

She stretched, using her free hand to reach the tray of Dr. Bernard's instruments. Her fingers fumbled over sharp, cold metal.

"You're safe," he murmured. His voice was a deep rumble in that heavily muscled chest as he assured her, "I'm not going to hurt you."

Macy couldn't make the same promise. A scalpel in her grasp, she lunged toward him. The hand on her mouth slid away. Then he caught her wrist in a tight grasp and knocked the weapon to the floor. The steel instrument thudded as it struck the linoleum.

She drew in a breath then released it in a high-pitched scream—not that anyone would hear her. The morgue was in the basement of the hospital and sound-proof because of the bone saw and other instruments Dr. Bernard used. But just in case Bob, the driver, had forgotten something and returned…

"Help! Help me!"

Although she struggled, the convict effortlessly man-acled both her wrists in one big hand and clamped the palm of his other hand over her mouth again. His fingers cupped the edge of her jaw, his thumb reaching nearly to the nape of her neck.

"Shh…"

Holding her, he swung his legs over the gurney and kicked off the bag with a barely perceptible shudder.

Although he'd lost his shirt somewhere, he wore jeans and prison-issue tan work boots. He was definitely an inmate—or he had been until his escape.

"No one's coming," he told her. "No one heard you scream."

Oh, God, now this man—*this escaped convict*—knew that he could do whatever he wanted to her. He held her in a tight grasp that she couldn't break despite how she struggled to free her wrists. Her weapon lay beyond her reach. She couldn't protect herself from him and she couldn't summon help.

Bob and Dr. Bernard would be returning. But would they come back from the prison in time to save her? This man hadn't gone to the trouble of escaping Blackwoods so he could hang around the county morgue. And if he was desperate enough to risk a prison escape, he was capable of anything.

Even murder…

Tears stung her eyes, but she blinked them back. She couldn't afford to lose it…not now. If she couldn't help herself, she wouldn't be able to help Jed.

She would be of no use to her brother…if she were dead.

His hand shaking with rage, Warden Jefferson James slammed the door to his private office. The force rattled the pictures on his wall, knocking his daughter's graduation portrait askew. He couldn't straighten it now; he couldn't even look at Emily. Her pale blond hair and big blue eyes reminded him so much of her mother. He hadn't been able to protect his wife from the real world. How had he thought he would be able to protect his daughter?

He turned his back on the wall of photos and stared out the window. The view of a cement wall topped with barbed wire rattled him, so he closed his eyes against it. He could leave here any time he wanted. Now. But he had to damn well keep it that way.

He dragged an untraceable cell phone out of his inside suit pocket and punched in a speed-dial number. "We have a problem."

"We?" his partner scoffed.

"Yeah, we," James snapped. "How the hell did you let an undercover DEA agent into Blackwoods?"

"You're the warden," he was needlessly reminded.

He knew, and at other times had relished, that he was the man in charge of one of the state's biggest penitentiaries.

"I can't turn prisoners away," he replied, not without raising more suspicions than Blackwoods apparently already had since it had become the target of a Drug Enforcement Administration investigation.

"You can't turn them away," his partner agreed, "but you can get rid of them. We agreed you were going to get rid of Rowe Cusack."

James ran his hand down his face, feeling the stubble and the lines and wrinkles of age and stress. "He left here in a body bag this morning."

A breath of surprise came over the phone. "I can't believe it was that easy for you to get rid of him," his partner admitted. "Cusack's one of the DEA's best agents."

"I'm not sure how easy it actually was," James admitted, bile rising in his throat along with fear and regret over what making sure Cusack was really dead had forced him to do. If only there had been another way...

"But you said he left in a body bag."

"Yeah, I'm just not sure he was really dead." Doc had declared him dead, but then the old physician had acted so strangely. So suspiciously...

Another breath rattled the phone, this time a gasp of fear. "You better make sure he's dead, or you have a problem."

"*We* have a problem."

"He doesn't know about my involvement, but he knows what's been going on in Blackwoods."

James glanced out the window again, at that damn cement wall and barbed-wire fence. "How—how do you know that he figured anything out?"

"Because he's a good agent and you just tried to kill him. He knows."

"He might be dead." That had been the plan, but had the plan really been carried out? James had seen all the blood on the floor of Cusack's cell, but that didn't mean the man had died from his wound.

"You better make damn sure he's really dead. Or..."

"Or what?"

"He won't be the only one dying," James's partner threatened.

A ragged sigh slipped through James's lips. How had everything gone so wrong? "He already isn't."

"You killed someone else?"

"*I* didn't kill anyone." His phone number was untraceable but he didn't trust that his partner wasn't recording the call. James had just learned how far he would go to cover his own ass; he suspected his partner would go just as far.

"You had someone else killed?"

He choked on the bile of his self-disgust. "I had to clean up the loose ends around here."

"You better concentrate on the biggest loose end. Cusack." His partner's voice rose with panic. "Make damn sure he's dead!"

The call disconnected, leaving Warden James with a dial tone and a pounding pulse. From the moment he had learned who the new inmate was, he'd known the DEA agent would prove dangerous. He just hadn't realized how dangerous Rowe Cusack was.

Chapter Two

Macy closed her eyes. Maybe this was just another nightmare. It couldn't be real. A dead body couldn't come to life. She had imagined the whole thing.

Dreamed it.

But when she opened her eyes, the prisoner was still there, his blue gaze trained on her face. "I'm going to take my hand away," he told her, his deep voice pitched low, "but I need you to stay calm."

He wasn't the only one. She needed to stay calm for herself, so she could figure out how to get the hell away from him and call authorities to apprehend him.

"Can you do that for me?" he asked.

She nodded.

"Not that you've been irrational," he admitted. "In fact you've been quite resourceful." His blue eyes narrowed as he studied her. Then he slid his hand down from her lips to cup her jaw, his palm warm against her skin. "You're smart."

She nodded again but remained silent. No one had heard her scream, so when she opened her mouth next, she needed to speak calmly and rationally and engage him in conversation without arousing his anger or distrust. She had to stall him until someone came—either Bob or Dr. Bernard.

After clearing the fear from her voice, she praised him. "You're smart, too. Very smart."

His lips curved into a slight grin, as if he were totally aware and amused by her tactic. "How do you know that?"

"No one has ever escaped Blackwoods before." She hadn't believed it possible or she might have considered using this ploy to help Jed escape.

"I didn't do it alone."

She glanced down at the empty body bag. "Someone else escaped with you?"

"Not with me. But he helped me."

"How?" she asked. "Tell me every detail." And in the time it would take him to brag about his successful plan, Dr. Bernard or Bob might return...if she were lucky.

And if she were very lucky, she might figure out a way to help her brother as well as herself. Maybe her helping apprehend an escaped convict would award Jed more privileges in prison, like more meetings with his lawyer in order to work on his appeal.

"You would like that," the man said, his grin widening, "you'd like to stall me until someone else shows up, someone who actually might hear you scream this time."

Was he going to give her a reason to scream? Did he intend to hurt her? Fear rushed back, choking her so that she couldn't deny the truth he spoke.

He nodded as if agreeing to something. "You are as smart as your brother said you are, Macy Kleyn."

Her pulse leaping at her name on his lips, she gasped. "Jed? You've talked to Jed?"

His handsome face twisted into a grimace, and he touched the bloodied bandage on his ribs. "Who do you think did this to me?"

She shook her head in denial, knocking his hand from her face. "Jed would not have done that to you. He would never hurt anyone."

She didn't care what a jury and a judge had decided; she knew her brother better than anyone else. He was not a killer.

"He had no choice," the man said, almost as if he were defending the guy he just claimed had stabbed him. "It was the only way to get me out of Blackwoods alive."

"By trying to kill you?" she asked.

"He didn't really try," he said. But besides the bandage, he had bruises on his ribs and one along his jaw. "He just made it look like he did. If your brother had really wanted me dead, I have a feeling that I wouldn't be talking to you right now. I'm lucky he came up with an alternative plan."

She reached for the bandage, her fingers tingling as they connected with his bare skin. She steadied her hand and tore off the gauze.

He grimaced as the stitches stuck to the dried blood, pulling loose. And a curse slipped through his clenched teeth.

"Who treated this?" she asked. "This needs more stitches." And antiseptic. The wound was too red, and as she touched it, too hot. He was going to develop an infection for certain.

"Doc just put in a couple quick stitches," he said, referring to the elderly prison doctor. "He couldn't do more without raising suspicions. It would have made no sense for him to treat a dead man."

"He declared you dead?"

He nodded. "And zipped me into that damn plastic bag before the coroner got to the prison."

"So the prison doctor and my brother both helped you escape Blackwoods?" she asked, careful to keep her doubts from her voice so that she wouldn't anger him. She had no idea how dangerous this man was. Given how delusional he was, she suspected that he was very dangerous.

"Yes," he replied, as if he actually expected her to believe him.

"It needs more stitches," she said, examining the wound, "it's too deep."

"Jed had to make it look believable, so I had to lose a lot of blood," he explained with a wince.

Just how much blood had he lost? Enough that he might be weak enough for Macy to be able to over-power him? But then she remembered how quickly he'd knocked the scalpel from her grasp. Muscles rippled in his arms and chest; he hadn't lost that much blood.

"None of this makes any sense." Jed would have never helped a convict escape prison. Dear sweet Doc, the prison doctor, wouldn't have helped either. This guy—whoever he was—was definitely lying.

She gestured toward the empty body bag. "I was supposed to toe tag you," she said. "What name would I have put on that?"

If he'd really been dead…

She would have looked at the records Dr. Bernard had sent with the body, but she couldn't reach for the file without his probably thinking she was reaching for a weapon again.

Although he didn't touch her now, she could still feel his hands on her wrists and her face. Her skin tingled where he had touched her and where she had touched him. She shouldn't have taken off his bandage, but she'd wanted to see the wound.

"Prison records will show my name is Andrew 'Ice' Johansen," he replied. After drawing in a deep breath, he continued, "But my real name is Rowe Cusack. I work for the DEA. I'm a drug enforcement agent."

She bit her bottom lip to hold in a snort of derision at this claim; it was nearly as wild as his claiming that Jed had stabbed him.

As close as they were standing, he didn't miss her reaction and surmised, "You don't believe me. Jed warned me that you wouldn't, that you're too smart and too suspicious to blindly accept my story."

"Can you prove it?" she challenged.

"I was undercover at Blackwoods Penitentiary. I couldn't exactly bring my badge and gun." He took in an agitated breath. "But my cover still got blown. Your brother knows who I am."

"How?"

"The warden told him…when he ordered Jed to kill me."

"No." She shook her head. "You're lying."

"Jed said you'd say that, too."

"Stop that!" she yelled, her patience snapping so that she could no longer humor him no matter how dangerous he was. "Stop quoting my brother to me. You don't know him."

"Not really," he agreed. "But I know about him like I know about you. I know that you were about to start med school when he got arrested, and you put off school for the trial. Then, after his sentencing to Blackwoods Penitentiary, you moved up here to be close to your brother. You believe in his innocence. But you're the only one."

She swallowed hard, choking on her doubts about this man's truthfulness. "I am the only one." Her ex-fiancé hadn't. Not even their parents had believed in Jed. But Macy had no doubt that her brother had been framed. "You haven't told me anything that you couldn't have found out from old newspaper articles."

During Jed's trial, the press had taken a special interest in her. Some had admired her sisterly devotion while others, including her ex-fiancé, had called her a fool for not accepting that her brother was a cold-blooded killer.

"How about this?" he challenged her. "You have a scar on the back of your head from when you fell out of Jed's tree house when you were seven."

She shivered, unnerved by the memory and more by the fact that this man knew it.

He continued, "There was so much blood that Jed thought for sure you were dead when he found you. But then you opened your eyes."

Like he had when she had unzipped the body bag. Now she understood how Jed had felt when she had done that all those years ago. He'd been kneeling by her side and when she'd opened her eyes, he had actually gasped. "Oh, my God…"

"That's not in any old newspapers," he pointed out. "Your brother told me that so you would believe me, Macy. He and I need you to believe me."

"You're really a DEA agent?" she asked, struggling to accept his words.

He leaned close to her, his forehead nearly brushing hers as he dipped his head. His gaze held hers. "I'm telling the truth. About everything."

Her world shifted, reduced to just the two of them—to his blue eyes, full of truth and something darker. Fear? Vengeance? She should have immediately recognized the emotion; she'd seen it before, in Jed's eyes, the day he had been sentenced to life—to two life sentences—in a maximum-security prison.

"Why does my brother want—*need*—me to believe you?"

"So you'll help me."

She drew in a shaky breath. "I'll help you," she agreed. "But only with your wound."

No matter what he was, she couldn't let him lose any more blood than he must have already lost. She reached for the tray of tools again.

He didn't stop her this time, not even when she began to add more stitches to the deep gash along his ribs. He just clenched his jaw and sucked up the pain, which had to be intense. She hadn't put even a local anesthesia on his skin, and she suspected the wound was getting infected. But he barely grimaced. The man had an extremely high threshold for pain.

"You need to call the Blackwoods county sheriff," she said. "Griffin York will be able to verify your story with the Drug Enforcement Agency."

"Administration," he automatically corrected her. Most people were probably not aware that the *A* actually stood for Administration and not Agency. But he would know—if he were truly a DEA agent. "Are you sure the sheriff's not on the warden's payroll?"

"No. I can't be sure," she admitted. "There are rumors that the warden made some pretty significant donations to the new sheriff's election campaign."

He groaned, probably not in pain but in frustration.

"You need to contact the Drug Enforcement Administration," she pointed out. And if he were really an agent, wouldn't he have already done that?

"I know for sure that someone with the DEA is on the warden's payroll," he said. "That's why I can't trust anyone. Nobody else can find out I'm still alive, or I'm a target."

She shrugged, feigning indifference. Even though she didn't know him and didn't trust him, she didn't want him to be killed. But helping a fugitive would land her in prison like her brother. And, unlike Jed, she wouldn't be innocent of the charges brought against her.

She probably shouldn't have treated this man's injury, but she had nearly become a doctor and as such, she would have taken an oath to do no harm. In Macy's opinion that included providing medically necessary treatment no matter the circumstances. After putting in the last stitch, she swabbed antiseptic on the wound. He sucked in a breath, and when she affixed the bandage, he covered her fingers with his.

"And if Warden James finds out I'm alive," Rowe continued, "then Jed's a dead man, too."

"Wh-why?" she sputtered as her greatest fear

gripped her. She tugged on her fingers, pulling them out from under his.

"Jed disobeyed the warden's order to kill me, and instead he helped me escape."

If Warden James had ordered Jed to kill another inmate, then her brother had become a liability to the man. Not that anyone would believe a convicted cop killer over a respected prison warden. But the warden might not be willing to take that chance. Nor would he want other prisoners believing they could get away with disobeying him.

The grinding of the descending elevator drew their attention to the open door of the morgue. "Is there another way out?" Rowe asked in an urgent whisper.

Macy shook her head. "There is no other way out of here."

"If I'm discovered and sent back to Blackwoods, I will be killed," he insisted, his blue eyes intense with certainty and desperation.

Damn it. She believed him and not just because of what he knew about her and her brother, but because he seemed too sincere to be lying. "And if you're killed, so will Jed…"

A door creaked open and a male voice called out, "Macy? You still here?"

"Y-y-yes, Dr. Bernard. I'll be out in a minute," she said. Then she rushed toward the wall and pulled open a drawer.

Rowe's dark gold brows drew together as he grimaced in revulsion. But he climbed inside the metal compartment. Macy threw a sheet over him. As she drew it up his bare chest, the backs of her fingers skimmed over skin and muscle. Her face heated, her blood pumping hard.

Rowe caught her wrist in his hand again. "Can I trust you?" he asked.

"If you're telling the truth, you don't have a choice," she said.

But despite knowing about the scar on the back of her head, was he really telling the truth? If he were actually a DEA agent, wouldn't he have been able to call *someone* to get him out of Blackwoods?

He released her wrist and drew in a deep breath as she pushed the drawer closed. But not tight.

"What are you doing?" Dr. Bernard asked.

Macy whirled toward her boss, stepping in front of the door behind which she'd hidden Rowe. "Wh-what do you mean?"

"I thought you'd be gone for the day by now." The doctor pushed a hand through his thin, gray hair. "I thought I'd be home by now."

"But you were called out to the prison again." For another body. Her pulse quickened. Had someone realized Rowe wasn't dead? And had they realized that Jed had helped him escape? "Wh-who was it…?"

"It was—it was…" His voice cracked with emotion. *God, not Jed…*

Dr. Bernard's hand shook as he pulled it over his face. "It was…Doc." He expelled a shaky breath. "Doc was killed."

Again she felt that quick flash of relief, which guilt and regret then chased away. "I'm sorry," she said. "I know he was a friend of yours."

"Even if he wasn't, nobody should die like that." The older man shuddered.

"Oh, my God—what happened?"

Dr. Bernard sighed. "I can determine cause of death even before I do a full autopsy. Someone beat him to death. What I can't tell you is—why."

"I'm sorry...."

His eyes glistened with a sheen of tears. "Why would someone do that to Doc?"

Maybe they had been trying to get information out of him. If they'd forced him to confess to declaring a live man dead, the coroner would probably be called out next for her brother. Her relief fled completely, leaving her tense and anxious.

"Bob's bringing Doc's body in, but the warden wants me to do the autopsy on that prisoner who died this morning first," Dr. Bernard said.

Nerves lifting goose bumps on her skin, Macy stepped away from the drawer. "Wouldn't the warden be more concerned about Doc?"

"You'd think. I know I am. I just don't know if I can autopsy him." Dr. Bernard shook his head, his gray eyes filling with sadness. "Too bad you hadn't gone to medical school. I could use an extra pair of hands around here."

"If I'd gone through medical school, you wouldn't be able to afford me," she teased, to lighten her boss's mood, like she always tried to lift Jed's spirits.

"True. And you're still my extra hands," Dr. Bernard said. And as a morgue assistant, she was much cheaper than a doctor. "Did you take a look at the prisoner?"

She nodded. "Cause of death is pretty obvious. Stab wound."

"So he's dead?"

She fought the urge to shiver. "I don't think he would've let me shut him in a drawer if he wasn't."

"Is that him?" He gestured toward the not-quite-shut drawer.

She shook her head. "No. That's Mr. Mortimer. The crematorium is coming to pick him up soon."

"That's why you're still here."

"I'll wait for Elliot." Elliot Sutherland worked at his uncle's crematorium/funeral home, but Elliot wasn't coming to the morgue. She had agreed to take the body to him, so that he and his band would not have to miss a gig. "And I'll wait for Bob to bring in Doc's body from the prison," she offered. "You go ahead home. The autopsies can wait till morning."

The coroner ran his hand over his face, etching the lines even deeper. "They're going to have to. The only cause of death I could figure out tonight would be my own. Exhaustion."

"Go home," she urged.

He offered her a halfhearted smile. "You've been a godsend, Macy. I'm not sure why you came to Blackwoods, but I'm really glad you did."

She could only nod. She would have rather been anyplace else. But she'd had no choice; she had to be close to Jed. He had no one else. And neither did she.

SHE HAD LEFT THE DRAWER OPEN a crack, but Rowe couldn't hear much. Her voice and the coroner's were muted, as if drifting down to him through six feet of dirt. Despite the coldness of the temperature inside the drawer and of the stainless steel against his bare back, sweat beaded on his skin, leaving it clammy.

Rowe fought the panic, just as he'd had to fight it while zipped inside the body bag. Jedidiah Kleyn's plan, to stab him deep enough to make it look fatal and convince the prison doctor to declare Rowe dead, had kept him alive but that damn plastic bag had nearly killed him.

Even though Doc had left it unzipped enough that he'd been able to draw some air, he'd had to force himself not to gasp. But then Macy Kleyn had unzipped him.

For a moment he'd thought she was an angel. She was so beautiful with her warm brown eyes and dark hair curling around a ponytail clip. Maybe she was an angel—a fallen one who'd brought him straight to hell when she'd shut him inside the drawer.

Although probably only minutes passed, it felt like hours. Then finally metal ground as the drawer opened and the sheet lifted from his face. He stared up—again—into those warm brown eyes. Rowe's stomach lurched. He shouldn't have let her shut him in the drawer where he hadn't been able to hear what she'd said to the coroner. Had she told her boss that the prisoner was alive? Were the warden and some of his guards about to burst into the morgue and drag him back to hell?

He reached out, grabbed the side of the metal wall and pulled out the drawer all the way. Then he sat up and swung one leg over the side. The ding of the elevator doors drifted back from the hall and had his every muscle clenching. At this hour, the morgue shouldn't be so busy. Employees wouldn't be coming and going. And no loved ones were coming to claim *his* body. She must have given him up for being alive—which was the same as giving him up for dead.

Rowe had been betrayed. Again.

Chapter Three

"Jed told me I could trust you," he said. Rowe had been a fool to believe a killer. But what choice had he had? His flimsy shiv hadn't even fazed the muscular giant, neither had any of the trick moves he'd learned growing up on the streets of Detroit.

He grimaced, his body aching from the well-placed blows Jed had used to subdue him. And the stab wound throbbed in spite of, or maybe because of, Macy's additional stitches.

If Rowe hadn't trusted the man, he would have wound up dead—at Jed's hands or another prisoner's. But still he shook his head in self-disgust. Someone in his own office must have betrayed him. So trusting a stranger, even though he hadn't really had any option, had been crazy.

"I should have known better than to believe a prisoner professing his innocence," he berated himself.

"Jed is innocent, and you can trust me," she assured him. Then she swung his leg back onto the tray and shoved him down.

"Get back in the drawer," she whispered, as footsteps approached with the squeak of rubber wheels rolling over tile.

"I'll be trapped in there," he said, the panic rushing over him again.

She shoved the drawer, sending it—and him—inside the cool cabinet. He hooked his toe so it wouldn't close all the way. But she must have been satisfied, because she scrambled into the hall. The wheels ground to a halt as she breathlessly told someone, "I got it."

What? Him?

Through the crack the drawer was left open, he studied the morgue, determining his escape route in case she had told the coroner the truth. But she walked back in alone—pushing a gurney.

He waited a moment, making sure no one else followed her. As if she had forgotten all about him, she just stood there and stared down at the body bag on the gurney. Breathing hard, he planted his palms against the top of the drawer and propelled the tray out the door.

"You okay?"

Her face pale and eyes wide and dark, she just shook her head. "No."

Son of a bitch…

Not her brother. Even if Jedidiah Kleyn wasn't innocent as he claimed, he didn't deserve to die like this just because he had helped Rowe instead of killing him.

"No…" he murmured, a knot of dread moving from his stomach to his chest. He jumped out of the drawer and walked over to the gurney. Then he reached for the zipper of the body bag and pulled it down, over the battered face of the man who had helped him.

But it wasn't Jed. It was the other man, the one who had been scared but agreeable to aiding Rowe's escape.

Rowe stared down at the bruised and broken body of the gray-haired prison doctor.

"Son of a bitch…" he cursed low and harshly. "I did this…."

As if rousing herself from a nightmare, Macy shook her head. "You were already on your way here in a body bag when this happened."

"But it's my fault," he said. "They beat him to death because of me."

Damn it. Damn it. If only there had been another way to get out…a way that hadn't involved an innocent man winding up dead.

"What if he told them you're not dead?" she asked, her voice cracking with fear. "Will my brother be coming here in the next body bag?"

"Macy—"

Anger flushed her face. "How could you use him like this? You put him in danger."

Just getting sentenced to Blackwoods had put Jedidiah Kleyn in mortal danger. More prisoners left like he had, in body bags, than on parole. That was part of the reason he'd been given his undercover assignment at the penitentiary. The other part of the reason had been the drugs that moved more freely than the bodies in and out of the prison.

"You have to help my brother," she pleaded. "You have to get him out before he winds up dead, too."

Rowe glanced down at Doc's battered face. If the elderly physician had talked, it was probably already too late for him to save Kleyn. The elevator dinged again, and Rowe groaned. Was this one her brother, just as she feared?

"I don't know who that is," Macy murmured, horror and dread glistening in her dark eyes. "It can't be…"

"It's not," he said.

"No," she agreed, and jerked her head in a nod that had her ponytail bouncing. "The van didn't have time to get to the prison and back again. It's not Jed."

Yet.

"Then it's someone you're not expecting."

She cursed and bit her lip. With a ragged sigh, she reached for the instrument tray and grabbed up a scalpel. She studied him a moment, as if she had just realized that the easiest way to save her brother was to prove that he had really killed the undercover DEA agent. Rowe's dead body would be all the proof she needed.

"I can't help your brother if I'm dead," Rowe pointed out.

"Get on a gurney," she whispered.

He hesitated a moment, wondering if she intended to plunge the scalpel into his chest the minute he lay down.

"Please," she murmured. "You have to—*your* life isn't the only one at risk now."

Hers was, too, just as Jedidiah Kleyn had worried would happen when Macy helped Rowe get out of the morgue. The *only* promise the prisoner had extracted in exchange for helping Rowe was that the DEA agent keep his little sister safe.

The sound of heavy footsteps echoing down the corridor compelled him to move. Whoever had come down to the morgue had not come alone. He had no more than jumped on a stretcher than Macy draped a sheet over him and pushed him into the hall. As she drew the morgue door shut behind them, the click of a lock echoed with finality. Through the sheet, he glimpsed shadows—several of them—walking toward the stretcher and Macy.

"Good evening, Warden James," she murmured. "How can I help you?"

By turning over the only man who had ever escaped Blackwoods Penitentiary and the corrupt warden's reign of terror?

MACY BIT HER LIP AND WISHED back her greeting. But the warden didn't react to her recognizing him. Everyone in Blackwoods County knew who Warden James was, so he probably would have reacted more had she pretended not to know him.

She held the scalpel beneath the edge of the gurney she clutched and realized how ineffectual the weapon was as she stared up at the broad-shouldered prison warden. With his bald head and big build, the fifty-something-year-old was an intimidating man. He didn't need the muscle he had brought with him, but four heavily muscled and armed guards stood behind him.

If they wanted to see the body under the sheet, she wouldn't be able to stop them, even with the scalpel. Her heart pounded hard and fast with fear that she had made a horrible mistake. She would have been smarter to lock her and the prisoner inside the morgue, rather than out of it.

"Get Dr. Bernard out here," Warden James said. The man was obviously used to everyone jumping to obey his commands.

If he had really ordered her brother to kill an under-cover agent, Jed would not survive his show of disobedience.

She swallowed hard and replied, "He left for the evening."

"Then you need to call him and get him back down here. Now," the warden insisted, a jagged vein standing out on his forehead as he barely contained his rage.

"I don't have the doctor's private numbers, and I'm not sure where he is, sir," she murmured, barely able to hear her own voice over the furious beating of her heart. Now she understood why everyone in Blackwoods County feared Warden Jefferson James whether they were confined in his prison or not.

"I'm just waiting for a funeral home pickup." Forcing away her nerves, she gestured with a steady hand toward the gurney.

"So you have a key to the morgue?"

She shook her head. It wasn't really a lie since she wasn't *supposed* to have a key to the morgue. "No. Dr. Bernard left me in the hall here, waiting. The funeral home's driver is late." Her friend wasn't actually going to show at all, but hopefully the warden wouldn't check her story.

"Who does have a key?" James persisted.

Despite the tension quivering in her muscles, she managed a shrug. "Maybe the hospital director?"

"Can you call him down here?"

She shook her head. "Sorry, sir, the phones don't even ring down here after hours. And I can't leave this body unattended until the funeral home gets here."

"Why not?" Warden James asked, his already beady

eyes narrowing with suspicion. "It's not like he's going to walk off."

A couple of his goons uttered nervous chuckles of amusement.

"Is it?" the warden asked. Now he focused on the DEA agent's sheet-covered body.

Macy willed the sheet not to move with Rowe's heartbeats or his breathing. "Of course not, sir. It's protocol for the hospital and the state that a body never be left unattended outside the morgue. I might lose my job if I leave." And her life if she stayed and the warden lifted that sheet. If he was willing to kill an undercover DEA agent, he would have no problem killing her. And then her brother...

Her eyes widened as she imagined the sheet shifting a bit as if sliding off Rowe's body, and she *accidentally* bumped into the gurney so that the wheels lurched a couple of inches across the linoleum floor. The sheet moved, too, but didn't slide off any farther. Nothing of Rowe was visible beneath it but the outline of his long, muscular body.

The warden stepped back with a slight shudder of revulsion. How could a man who was so often around death be unnerved by it? "I don't give a damn about protocol," he said. "I need to talk to your boss right now."

"If you go to the main desk upstairs, they can help you," she said. "They'll be able to reach Dr. Bernard at home and have him come back to the morgue."

The warden glared at her before turning and heading toward the elevator. Like devoted dogs at his heels, the guards followed him. Macy waited until the doors closed on him and his henchmen; then she exhaled the breath she'd held and her knees weakened. She stumbled against the gurney and sent the wheels rolling forward a few feet this time.

Still covered with the sheet, the body rose, like a ghost rising from the dead. Then Rowe shrugged off the shroud and turned to her. He expelled a ragged sigh as if he'd been holding his breath. "That was close."

"That was crazy," she said, trembling in reaction to the confrontation. "I thought for sure he was going to lift the sheet. You were moving." She reached out to smack him, as she would have her brother, but this man wasn't her brother. He was a potentially dangerous stranger, so she snatched back her hand before she could connect with his bare skin and muscle.

"I wasn't moving," he said, his already impressive chest expanding as he filled his lungs. "I wasn't even breathing."

In her fear, she had only imagined the sheet slipping then. "The warden kept staring at you like he knew I was lying…."

Thank God he had not called her on that lie.

"I thought your brother was lying," Rowe admitted.

"About his innocence?" She bristled with indignation. "He *is* innocent."

"I thought he was lying, or at least exaggerating about you," he said, as he slid off the gurney, "but you are *really* smart. You think faster on your feet than some agents with years of experience on the job."

"I feel like a fool," she said, because he was probably playing her for one. "I should have called the police, or at least told Dr. Bernard about you." She could have trusted her boss to help her; he had treated her very well the past three years.

"You'll get me and your brother killed," Cusack warned her.

"I only have your word that will happen," she pointed out. And she had been stupid to take his word for anything.

"Remember what happened to Doc," he advised her. "Why do you think he died?"

"I don't know," she said. "It could have had nothing to do with you. A prisoner could have freaked out on him." So many ODs came to the morgue from the prison, the inmates overdosing on controlled substances to which they never should have had access. It was very plausible and overdue for the DEA to investigate the drug problem at Blackwoods Penitentiary.

"Then why did the warden show up here?" he asked, his blue eyes bright with anger. "He's looking for me."

"And I probably should have turned you over to him." But she couldn't take the risk that Jed wouldn't get hurt or, worse, wind up like Doc, if she talked.

Trusting this stranger, though, was putting her own life at risk. Warden James was not going to be happy if he learned that she had lied to him. So she had to make certain that he never learned the truth.

"I THINK YOUR BROTHER DID kill me and send me straight to hell," Rowe grumbled as he zipped up the sweatshirt Macy had tossed over the seat a minute before. "First a body bag and a coroner's van."

"Then a slab in the morgue," she murmured over her shoulder.

"And a cold unventilated drawer." It had also been dark and confining, reminding him of those closets he'd been locked in so many years ago.

"I didn't shut it all the way."

He leaned through the partition separating the back from the front seat. "No, you didn't, or I would have suffocated and wouldn't be taking this ride right now—" Rowe shook his head in disbelief "—in the back of a hearse."

"You couldn't just walk out of the morgue," Macy said, her voice muffled as she stared straight ahead, peering through the windshield. She steered the hearse down the narrow road which, like every other road in Blackwoods County, wound around woods and small, inland lakes in the Upper Peninsula of Michigan.

"No, I couldn't, not with Warden James and his goons hanging around the hospital," he agreed. So he'd had to trust Macy Kleyn again and rely on her quick-witted thinking to get him out of the hospital unseen.

He lifted his gaze from the windshield to the rear-view mirror hanging from it, and caught the reflection of headlamps burning through the darkness behind them. His gut knotted with apprehension. "But someone still might have followed us."

In the rearview, Macy's wide-eyed gaze met his. "Someone's following us?"

"It's possible." Given his recent run of bad luck, highly probable.

"Or maybe you're just paranoid," she said, her voice light even though her eyes, reflecting back at him from the rearview mirror, darkened with fear.

"Paranoia isn't necessarily a bad thing." He touched

the wound on his ribs that Macy had had to add stitches to completely close. If her brother had obeyed the warden, that knife would have gone deep enough to kill Rowe.

Who within the administration had given him up? His handler or someone else in the office? He had worked with his handler, Agent Jackson, before. Hell, after six years with the DEA, he had worked with everyone in his department and a few others. He would have never suspected one of the special agents of blowing someone's cover. But it was the only way the warden could have learned his real identity.

So Rowe had no idea who he could trust—besides Macy Kleyn. And if he'd gotten her brother killed, he was certain she would turn on him, too. "Because sometimes everybody really is out to get you."

"I know." She jerked the wheel, abruptly turning off the road. The hearse barely cleared the trees on either side of it as it bounced over the ruts of a two-track road. She shut off the lights but not the engine as she continued, blind, through the trees.

"Where the hell did you learn to drive like this?" he asked, that paranoia making him suspicious of her now. Her brother had said she was studying to become a doctor, not a stunt driver.

"EMT class."

"So how did you wind up working in the morgue?" he asked, with a sense of revulsion as he remembered the coldness and the closeness of that drawer she'd kept shutting him in.

"I applied for a job as an ambulance driver," she explained, "but the only opening at the hospital was in the morgue."

She had given up school and her choice of career to be close to her brother—a brother Rowe might have gotten killed just as he had Doc.

Remembering the frustration and worry in his voice when Jed had told him about his younger sister, Rowe said, "Now that we're away from the hospital, you need to drop me off somewhere and then forget that you ever saw me."

She snorted out a breath that stirred her bangs. "Not likely."

"Macy, I appreciate what you've done, but I can't ask you to do any more." He couldn't allow her to get involved any deeper than she already was. He wouldn't break his promise to the man who had gotten him out of Blackwoods alive.

"I'm not doing this for you," she said as she pulled up behind a building. After shutting off the engine, she jumped out. Seconds later the back door of the hearse opened. Moonlight glinted off a row of smokestacks on the corrugated steel roof.

"Where the hell are we?" he asked as he crawled out of the hearse.

"Hell is right." She tossed his earlier words back at him. "The crematorium." She jangled a ring of keys in her palm.

"You have the keys?"

"It's my second job," she explained. *"Unofficially."*

"That's why the hearse was in the parking lot?" He'd been surprised when she had rolled his gurney out to that particular vehicle.

"Yes, Elliot took my van and left the hearse. We have an arrangement."

"And that is?" And who the hell was Elliot?

"I fill in for him when he has a gig. He's a musician. He pays me cash, and I don't tell his dad, who owns this place, that Elliot's not doing his job." Her teeth flashed in the moonlight as she smiled.

"Nice arrangement—if neither of you mind a little blackmail."

"What's a little blackmail between friends?" she said with another quick smile and a shrug. "It's going to work out well for you."

"It already has. You got me past the warden." He glanced back toward the road, but he could see nothing other than the dark shadow of leafless trees swaying in the cool night breeze. Yet if someone had been following them, they may have just shut off their lights, too.

Were they sneaking up on them now? He had no weapon, nothing to defend himself and her. Lying under that sheet in the morgue had been the hardest thing he'd ever done—relying on her to protect them both. Her brother hadn't exaggerated about her at all. Macy Kleyn was damn smart.

Too smart to be risking her life for him.

Macy rattled the keys as she fingered through them, obviously searching for the right one. "Are you warm enough in the sweatshirt?" she asked as she huddled in her parka.

Winter was officially over, but northern Michigan had yet to get the memo. Rowe ignored the wind biting through the shirt to chill his skin. He had more to worry about than the weather.

"I'm fine. Thanks."

"It's freezing out. Elliot might have a coat inside," she said. Finally, she jammed a key in the lock and pushed open the back door.

He hesitated outside. Even though it was damn cold, he would rather be out in the open than confined anywhere else. Ever. Again.

"What are we doing here?" he asked.

"We're going to burn the wrong body."

"What?" He glanced back to the hearse. He had made damn certain that he'd been riding alone back there. While he'd done his share of skeevy undercover assignments, this one had been the stuff of horror movies since the first moment the prison bars had slid closed behind him. And it had only gotten worse since he'd escaped. "Whose body are we going to burn?"

"Yours."

He laughed at her outrageous comment. "Yeah, right. You're funny, too." Kleyn hadn't shared that tidbit about his kid sister.

"I'm not kidding."

"Then you're crazy."

Her teeth flashed in a quick smile. "You're not the first one to call me that."

When she flipped on a light, he studied her. "Have you been called that because you believe your brother is innocent?"

She jerked her head in a sharp nod.

"And because you quit school to move up here to be close to him?"

"That wasn't about being close to him," she clarified. "It's about proving his innocence."

"That may be impossible to prove," he warned her. No matter how smart Macy Kleyn was, she wouldn't be able to prove the innocence of a guilty man.

"Alone," she admitted. "It would be. That's why I want…" Her gaze skimmed up and down his body, over the black sweatshirt that molded like a second skin to his chest and over the faded jeans.

If she kept looking at him like that, Rowe had a feeling he would give her whatever she wanted. "Are you going to tell me or do I have to guess? I don't have time for games, Macy."

He had already wasted too much time that he should have spent putting distance between him and Blackwoods Penitentiary. A lot of distance.

"I know," she agreed. "So lie down."

His heart kicked his ribs. Maybe he really had died, but he'd gone to heaven instead of hell…if Macy Kleyn wanted him. "What? Why?"

"Lie down on this," she said, and pointed toward a metal table. "And play dead again."

"We're out of the morgue," he reminded her.

"But we're not done yet." She picked up a Polaroid camera.

He had trusted her before and she hadn't betrayed him. Yet. With a sigh, Rowe lay down. "I'm getting a little too good at playing dead."

"We have to do this right, or you won't just be playing."

"We?" There she went with the word Rowe had always made a point of never using. "I just needed your help to get out of the morgue. I don't need anything else from you."

"Really?" she asked, her lips curving into a smug smile. "Do you have a cell phone? Someone to call if you did? A ride or a vehicle to take you somewhere Warden James won't find you? Or the police who will be looking for you when news of your escape from prison gets out?"

He clenched his jaw so hard his teeth ground together. She was right. He had none of those things. No one he could trust. But he had made a promise. "I'll figure it out."

"I'll help you."

"You're not even convinced I'm telling you the truth," he said. She was too smart to completely trust him despite his knowing about her childhood accident.

"But if you are telling the truth and I don't help you, I'll never forgive myself."

"What happens to me is not your responsibility," he said. No one had ever really taken responsibility for him. Not his parents and now not even the handler who should have pulled him out weeks ago when he hadn't heard from Rowe.

"No, it's not," she agreed. "But I would never forgive myself for wasting this opportunity to help Jed, too."

He narrowed his eyes at her. He suspected she wasn't talking about just keeping her brother out of trouble with the warden. "What do you want?"

"Close your eyes."

He, who had always had problems with authority, did as she said. And a light flashed behind his lids.

He sprang up. "What are you doing?"

"Shut up. Dead men don't talk."

Chapter Four

Dead men didn't do a lot of things that Rowe couldn't help but think of doing with her, especially as her hands pressed against his shoulders, pushing him back onto the table.

"Don't look so tense," Macy directed him. "Relax."

"You're not the one somebody's trying to kill." Not yet anyway. But once the warden figured out Macy had helped Rowe get out of the morgue—and the man was too shrewd not to figure it out—he would retaliate. First by killing her brother and then...

"Macy, I appreciate everything you're doing," he sincerely told her, "but you can't help me. I can't get you any more involved than you already are. It's too dangerous."

"I'm already involved," she pointed out as she snapped another picture. "So I might as well get something for my trouble."

Disappointment rose like bile in his throat. Macy Kleyn was certainly no angel; just like everyone else, she had her price.

He asked her again, "What do you want?"

"I will help you get in contact with someone you can

trust," she said, "someone who can get you safely out of Blackwoods County."

That was easier said than done, and his wish, not hers. "And what do you want in exchange?"

"For you to get Jed safely out of Blackwoods Penitentiary."

"You want me to break your brother out of prison?" he asked. Apparently she still hadn't accepted that Rowe was a federal agent, since she expected him to break the law for her.

"I want you to clear his name," she said. Her hands gripped his shoulders again, squeezing. "He was framed."

Rowe sat up and swung his legs over the side of the metal table, his thigh bumping against her hip. Unable to help himself, he touched her again, cupping her soft cheek in his palm. His fingers tunneled into her hair, brushing over the ridge of the scar on the back of her head. Her eyes, so full of intelligence, widened as she stared up at him.

Rowe couldn't lie to her even though Jed probably had, so that he wouldn't lose her respect and adulation. "Everybody serving time in jail claims that they've been framed."

"Even you," she said, her chin lifting defensively as she pulled away from him and stepped out of his reach.

"I wasn't framed," he clarified. "A jury did not find me guilty of any crime. A judge did not sentence *me* for any crime. I was sent in undercover to investigate Blackwoods."

"A cover that didn't last long."

He didn't need the reminder. His ribs ached, the

wound throbbing. But he welcomed the pain; it confirmed that he was still alive. For now.

"Why was that?" she asked. "Aren't you very good at what you do?"

"I'm the best," he said. He wasn't just bragging, either; he had the commendations to prove it. But more importantly he had the convictions. He had put away so many bad people. After seeing how the prison doctor had been tortured and beaten, he suspected that the warden might prove the worst. Rowe had to put him away, but he couldn't do that if the warden found him first. "Someone blew my cover."

"Who?"

"I don't know." He looked away from her, then back again to her beautiful face. "And that's why I can trust no one." Not even her.

"You can trust me, Rowe," she promised, her big brown eyes earnest.

"No, I can't."

She smiled slightly, as if pitying him. "I don't think you have a choice."

Rowe was afraid that she was right. Maybe about everything. "You really believe that your brother was framed?"

She studied him a moment before nodding. "Just like I believe that you're really an undercover DEA agent."

He closed his eyes, dragged in a deep breath then committed himself. "Okay, we have a deal."

Her eyes widened and sparkled with hope. "You'll help Jed?"

"*If* he was really framed, I'll work to clear his name," Rowe promised.

But in making this vow to Macy, he was breaking his promise to her brother. The more help Rowe accepted from her, the more danger he put her in.

"He was framed," Macy insisted with total certainty.

Her brother had to be telling the truth, because if he really was a cop killer, he would have killed Rowe instead of risking his own life to get him out. A killer wouldn't have hesitated to kill again. Only a good man would put himself in danger to save someone else.

"Then I have to help him." Because Rowe knew what it felt like to be an innocent man locked up like an animal. He had only been behind bars for weeks; Jed had been sentenced to life, which might not be a bad thing if Rowe wound up getting his sister killed. Because if that happened, Rowe had no doubt that Jed would really become a killer.

"You can't help anyone if you're dead, though," Macy said, as if she'd read his mind. "So I'm going to fire up the incinerator now."

"The what?"

"The oven," she said, gesturing toward the big metal box at the end of the metal table. "We have to burn your body."

God, she really was crazy. And he had actually considered trusting her....

JEFFERSON JAMES SHOVED THE coroner aside and dragged open those refrigerated steel drawers, himself, until every damn one was pulled completely out of the wall. Only a few held bodies. An old man. A teenage accident victim.

Doc.

He quickly looked away from the battered face of the man he had once considered a friend. Or if not a true friend, at least an ally. For years Doc had had no problem cashing his very generous payroll checks. He'd known why his salary was so much higher than any other prison doctor's. He had been reimbursed for his discretion. But then he'd taken it too far.

He'd betrayed James. And no one betrayed Jefferson James and lived to brag about it.

"Where is he?" the warden snapped, his anger and frustration spilling over.

Where the hell was Rowe Cusack?

Bernard gazed around the room, as if the body was hiding somewhere in the white-tiled room. He ran a hand over his face, wiping away the last traces of sleep. James had had to wake him up and physically drag him out of bed to bring him back to the morgue.

It was late. But James didn't care. He wasn't sleeping himself until he saw Rowe Cusack's dead body with his own damn eyes.

"Bob brought the prisoner's body straight here from Blackwoods," Dr. Bernard said.

"Then where the hell did it go?" the warden asked. "Did he get up and walk out the damn door?" He tensed, goose bumps lifting on his skin as he realized what he'd said and that he'd said it before. His men, the guards who stood in the doorway between the morgue and the outer office, didn't chuckle this time.

"I don't know why you're so worried about this prisoner," Bernard said. "You're acting like he's not dead. But that's not possible. Doc declared him dead." He glanced toward his friend's body. The two physicians had been true friends.

How much did Bernard know about what went on in Blackwoods? With the bodies that came from the prison to the morgue, he had to know…too much.

James followed Bernard's gaze to Doc's body. Why would the old man have risked their financially beneficial arrangement and his life? How had Cusack gotten to him?

"And since Doc declared that guy dead, he's dead," Bernard insisted.

James's voice shook with rage now as he shouted, "Then show me his damn body! Now!"

The coroner walked over to the wall of open drawers as if Cusack was hiding somewhere inside it. But the man had been too damn big to just disappear. He would have filled one of those drawers. Or covered a whole damn gurney, like that body the girl had been standing next to earlier. She and that body were gone now.

"The crematorium was coming for this body," Bernard said, stopping next to the drawer holding the old man. "They must have taken the wrong one."

"The crematorium?" Warden James asked. "The girl that was here earlier said she was waiting for the funeral home."

"The crematorium is part of Sutherland's funeral home," Bernard explained. "Sutherland's kid works for him. He would have been the one coming to pick up the body to be cremated."

"So you're saying that if his body went there, by mistake, that it's going to be burned?" Leaving behind no proof that the man had ever existed? That wouldn't necessarily be a bad thing, if James didn't doubt that the man was actually dead.

"Yes. But probably not until tomorrow. We will be able to retrieve the prisoner's body for you, Warden," Bernard assured him. "Don't worry."

But he couldn't stop worrying…until he knew for sure that DEA Agent Rowe Cusack was dead and not about to destroy James's entire operation.

MACY WAS CRAZY. She had made a lot of sacrifices for Jed, quitting med school, moving to Blackwoods County, working two jobs…

But this, helping Rowe Cusack, could prove to be her greatest sacrifice yet. Maybe the ultimate sacrifice. Her hands trembling, she tightened her grip on the steering wheel. "You're sure Elliot didn't see you?"

"Only the Polaroid you showed him of my body," Rowe answered from the back of her van. He lay across the seats with his head low so that she couldn't even catch a glimpse of him in the rearview mirror.

All she spied were the headlamps of another vehicle burning through the thick darkness behind her. Did that vehicle just happen to be on the road leading toward the small cabin she rented? Or had it been following her since she'd left the hospital?

"Good," she said. "Then if anyone asks about you at Sutherland's, he will vouch that you were cremated tonight."

"It was a great idea, Macy." He praised her with none of the surprise other people had showed in her intelligence.

She felt empowered. She enjoyed actually being able to help someone for once instead of being forced to stand by while he was unjustly imprisoned. Yet still she worried....

What if Rowe Cusack wasn't really whom he claimed to be? Not only would he be unable to help her brother but she'd have just aided and abetted an escaped convict. But Jed would have never revealed that childhood story unless he had been sending her a message.

"You've helped me more than I could have imagined," he said, as if he'd never met anyone who had helped him without an agenda. He still hadn't, though. She had an agenda...for Jed. "I can't ask you to do any more."

Her breath caught in alarm. "You're backing out of our arrangement?"

"No. I'll help Jed," he promised. Again.

Dare she believe him? She had once been naive enough to believe what people told her, to believe in justice and fairness. She had learned three years ago to trust in no one and nothing. Except her brother.

"But I can't do anything for anybody until I figure out who blew my cover and why," Rowe continued, his deep voice vibrating with anger.

"You really have no idea?"

"I don't know who to trust in the DEA," he said. "Not anymore. And I know I can't trust anyone in Blackwoods."

"Except Jed." But was Jed still in prison, or was he headed to the morgue for disobeying the order to kill the DEA agent? Hopefully Macy had done enough to cover Rowe's and Jed's tracks.

A short chuckle emanated from the backseat. "Jedidiah Kleyn is the last person I would have thought I could trust in that hellhole."

"Why?"

"That whole cop killer thing," he reminded her.

She grimaced at the horrific charges against her brother. Being accused of killing a police officer—being convicted of it—had nearly destroyed Jed, who'd just returned from a tour in Afghanistan where he'd been training Afghanis to become police officers.

"It's why the warden ordered Jed to carry out the hit on me," Rowe continued.

"But he's innocent." Frustration that she was the only one who believed it had tears stinging her eyes. She blinked them back, having learned long ago that crying accomplished nothing.

"Innocent or not, he's still as intimidating as hell," Rowe informed her. "Nobody messes with your brother. Nobody dares."

"Jed doesn't tell me much." And she hated that; she had moved close to him so that he would have someone he could count on, someone he could talk to. Yet he wouldn't talk to her except to urge her to go back to her home and life. Back to school. And she always assured him that she would, as soon as he was able to go back to his home and his life. "He doesn't want to worry me, but I know Blackwoods is hell."

"And the warden is the devil," Rowe said. Unlike Jed, he didn't coddle her.

She appreciated his honesty. God, she hoped he was

telling the truth about helping Jed. "Yours wasn't the first body to come to the morgue from the prison."

And every time Bob had wheeled a body bag into the morgue, she had lived a waking nightmare of worry that it was Jed.

"Mine wasn't even the only body today," Rowe said, his deep voice thick with regret as he obviously thought of the torture Doc had endured. Over him.

"It's not your fault," she tried to convince him. He had appeared as horrified unzipping Doc's body bag as she must have looked unzipping his. "You can't blame yourself for Doc dying."

"No. But I'm going to find out whose fault it is," he vowed. "Warden James isn't acting alone. I want to know who else is to blame."

"The warden has to be stopped," she said, her heart aching with concern for Jed. "Too many inmates die in Blackwoods. They've been shivved. Or beaten to death. Or they've overdosed on drugs they never should have been able to get."

"I was put undercover in Blackwoods because of the number of ODs," he explained. "It's obvious there's a big problem. Someone's been bringing drugs into the prison."

With her old naïveté, she wouldn't have believed they'd be able to get them inside, but now she knew anything was possible. Especially horrible things. "They shouldn't be getting them past the guards."

"No, they shouldn't," Rowe agreed, his voice sharp with anger.

"How long have you been inside?" she asked.

"Just a few weeks."

"Jed's been in for three years." And while she knew her brother had it so much worse, sometimes she felt like she was in prison, too. Her life—the one she had planned since she'd been a little girl—had ended with his sentence. He had been furious with her for not going to medical school, and he hadn't wanted her to move either. But he'd had no one else.

Their parents had turned their backs on him, just as they had once turned their backs on her. They hadn't understood her learning disability and had written her off as stupid. But Jed had never doubted her intelligence, and as a teenager, he had researched on his own to figure out his baby sister was dyslexic. He had believed in *her* when no one else had.

"Three years is a *long* time in Blackwoods," Rowe remarked with a soft whistle.

"I've been trying to get him out," she said. "But I can't do it on my own. And you can't figure out who betrayed you on your own. You need my help."

"No, Macy," Rowe insisted. "You've already done too much. You've gotten too involved. I can handle it from here."

She tightened her grip on the steering wheel. The helplessness she'd felt when her brother was sentenced to life flashed through her. She hadn't been able to help him, but she could help Rowe, if he would let her. "You need me. I—"

Bright lights, glinting off the rearview mirror, blinded her. The vehicle behind them had sped up and closed the distance between them. No brakes squealed. It didn't try to stop or pass. Instead it plowed right into the back of the van, which jumped forward from the impact.

Rowe's body thumped against the back of her seat and a string of curses slipped from his lips. "I was right. We were followed from the hospital."

"They're not just following anymore," she said, shifting forward on the old bucket seat so that she could press her foot down harder on the accelerator. The van's tires squealed as she careened around a sharp curve.

Rowe moved between the seats as if to climb into the front, but she pried one trembling hand from the steering wheel to shove him back.

"Stay down!" she yelled. "They might see you."

"You don't think they already know I'm in here?" he asked, his voice rough with irony and frustration.

A lawman would be used to protecting others, not relying on others to protect him. If he really was the DEA agent she was pretty certain that he was, then this had to be killing him almost as much as the warden wanted him killed.

But she couldn't let him carry all the guilt, not when this might have nothing to do with him at all.

"We don't know if these people are after you," she said, grasping the wheel with both hands as she maneuvered around another corner. The van shifted, as if the wheels left the asphalt. She couldn't lose control, not now when she was gaining distance between them and whatever vehicle pursued them.

"If they're not after me, then who are they after?" Rowe asked.

She swallowed hard and then choked out the admission. "Me."

"WHY WOULD ANYONE be after you?" Rowe asked. Finally. He had saved the question until she'd lost whatever vehicle had been chasing them. Had she really learned to drive like that from an EMT course, or because she'd once been a wheelman—wheel person? She drove more like a get-away driver than an ambulance driver. Rowe suspected there was more to Macy Kleyn than her big brother knew.

She tugged on the ropes of the blinds, dropping them down over the night-darkened windows of the small cabin to which she'd driven him once she had lost their tail.

The impenetrable blackness of a moonless night enveloped the cabin and the woods surrounding it. Anyone could have been out there, hiding in the dark, watching them. So even with the blinds closed, he caught her hand when she reached for the lights.

"Why would anyone be after you?" he asked again, tightening his grasp when she tried to tug free. "What are you involved in?"

Was she part of the corruption at Blackwoods? She had a man on the inside, and she could have been using her autonomy at the morgue to cover up prison breaks like his as well as other crimes. Like all those inmates who'd died of overdoses...

Self-disgust filled him that he had begun to trust her. But just like with her brother, he hadn't had any other option. Until now. He had no reason to stay with her... except the promise he'd made to her brother to keep her safe.

"Despite his innocence, my brother's been labeled a cop killer," she said. "Some people aren't too happy that I'm trying to help him appeal those charges and overturn his sentence."

"You've been threatened before?"

She sighed, her breath whispering across his skin as they stood close. "Yes. Stupid things like my tires getting slashed or my windows broken."

"Has anyone tried running you off the road before?"

She nodded, or at least the dim shadow of her nodded. "Yes. Not here in Blackwoods, but it happened a couple of times back home."

"Did you file a report?"

"It was a police car."

He cursed.

"That's why we can't be certain that the vehicle that bumped into the van tonight had anything to do with you," she finally explained.

"We can't be certain that it didn't." And that was why he couldn't leave. He had made a promise to her brother that he intended to keep; Macy Kleyn would not be hurt because of him.

"Then it's even more important to find out who gave you up," she said, "so that we can be certain."

"You understand that I can't help Jed until I find that out?" he asked. If he couldn't help himself, he wouldn't be able to help anyone else.

She stepped closer, her eyes shining in the dark as she stared up at him. "That's why you need me."

His muscles tightened, reacting to her words and her proximity. She stood so close that her thighs nearly brushed against his. Heat emanated from her, chasing the chill from his body. What the hell was wrong with him that he wanted this woman—this stranger—so badly?

He had only been inside for three weeks, not three years like her brother. And damn, knowing her brother, he'd have to be crazy to give in to his attraction to Macy Kleyn. He finally released her wrist and stepped back, needing some distance between them.

"I've been with the DEA for six years, Detroit P.D. four years before that," he informed her. "I know how to handle an investigation. I don't want you involved in this."

"It's too late."

That was what he was afraid of.

"We'll talk about this in the morning," she said, as if she were his handler and not Agent Jackson.

He probably wouldn't be in this mess if she had been his handler. Would Donald Jackson really have betrayed him though? Rowe had known the man so long and had always believed he could trust him explicitly. They had the same background, the same reasons for caring so damn much about their jobs.

But maybe that had burned Jackson out, that no matter how hard they worked it wasn't ever enough to get all the drugs off the streets. Maybe that was why he'd turned...

"We'll figure out our next step then," she said.

If Rowe were smart, he would be gone before morning. He would steal her keys, her van and her cell phone. And never see her again.

"I'll make up the couch for you and find you something to wear," she offered. "I brought Jed's stuff along when I moved up here." Her brother's sentence was life for each life he'd taken: two consecutive life sentences. He wouldn't need his things anymore. But Macy was that determined to free him, despite the threats to her own safety.

"You live here year-round?" he asked.

The cabin was small and had probably been intended for short hunting trips only. He doubted that it had a furnace, since the place was so cold he could nearly see her breath when she replied.

"Yes. It has indoor plumbing and a fireplace that I need to light so that the plumbing won't freeze. The blinds are room darkening and very private. No one will be able to see inside." She didn't wait for his permission now. She turned on a lamp and then struck a match to the kindling in the old fieldstone fireplace.

"How does that heat the whole place?" Rowe asked, but then he saw that except for one door leading to the bathroom, the place was only one room. Her bed was against one wall, the couch at the foot of it. He was to sleep there? Within feet of her?

She followed his gaze to the old brass bed. "Don't worry. I won't take advantage of you."

He chuckled. "I'm used to sleeping with one eye open." Even more so since his last undercover assignment had sent him to Blackwoods Penitentiary.

"I'm used to sleeping with a gun under my pillow," she said, obviously putting him on notice not to try anything. "And I know how to shoot."

She opened a cabinet, pulled out a pair of flannel pajama bottoms and a thermal shirt and tossed them at him.

He caught the clothes and dropped them onto the old

leather couch. Even if it wasn't so close to where she would be sleeping, he doubted he would be able to get any rest on the worn leather stretched over lumpy cushions. She picked up the clothes and handed them back to him as she laid flannel sheets and a flannel comforter over the couch.

"You can use the bathroom first," she said. "The water heater works really well, so the shower's hot."

A shower, without having to watch his back, sounded like heaven. But it didn't matter that he was out of prison; he still needed to watch his back, maybe especially around Macy Kleyn. Was she really armed? "They didn't teach you how to shoot in EMT class."

"No," she replied. "Jed taught me."

"Of course."

Remembering how protective and how damn big her brother was reined in Rowe's desire when later that night she stepped from the bathroom wearing only a short flannel nightgown. She wasn't that tall, but her legs were long and slender. Her hair was down and loose around her shoulders, firelight reflecting in the dark silky waves. Why did she have to be as beautiful as she was smart?

He closed his eyes, but her image was still there, behind his lids, taunting him just as the bed springs did when she crawled beneath her blankets. At least he hoped she was beneath them, every tempting inch of her covered up.

He'd kicked off his blankets. He'd blamed the proximity of the fireplace for making him too hot. But it had been the shower running and knowing that Macy stood naked beneath the water that had overheated him.

If he'd been smart, he would have taken her keys then and snuck out while she'd been in the bathroom.

But after having to stay low and out of sight in the van, he had no idea what streets she'd taken from the crematorium to her cabin or from the hospital to the crematorium. And he would never figure it out at night. He would wait until morning and then he'd leave.

He forced his body to relax. Even though the couch was too short, it was still more comfortable than the prison cot. And while he shouldn't trust her any more than he had his inmates at Blackwoods, he did. She might be keeping secrets, but he doubted she was a killer, despite the gun. Knowing she was armed actually eased his mind. He didn't have to worry about protecting her, not when she so capable of protecting herself.

For the first time in three weeks he drifted off to sleep. He might have slept for minutes or maybe even hours before the rapid cracks of gunshots jerked him awake.

Chapter Five

Strong hands gripped Macy's shoulders, pulling her from her pillow and her slumber. He had been there in her dream, just as he was now. Shirtless, which left his muscular chest bare but for the soft-looking golden hair that narrowed to an arrow above his washboard abs. The too-big pajama bottoms rode dangerously low on his lean hips, so low that she forced her gaze back up to his face. His blond hair was rumpled, and brownish-blond stubble darkened his square jaw.

His icy-blue eyes stared deeply into hers. "Macy?"

She blinked, but his image didn't clear from her mind. He was there. In her bed. What could he want with her...?

"Where's your gun?"

She laughed—at herself and her wild imagination more than his question.

"Didn't you hear those shots?" he asked with impatience and anger. "Someone's out there firing at us."

"More than likely they're firing at a deer or a rabbit." She never kept track of which season it was, but then the "official" hunting seasons didn't matter much in Blackwoods County. Whether it was legal or not, someone was always killing something.

"Give me the gun," he directed her, "and I'll check it out."

She blinked the sleep from her eyes and forced herself to focus on more than his chest. "No. It could be a trap."

He pushed a hand through his sleep-tousled hair. "Yeah. They could be using the shots to draw me outside."

She nodded. "Like I said, it's probably just a hunter...."

He arched a dark gold brow. "And I'm what they're hunting?"

"It's always open season on an escaped convict."

"Exactly. That's why I need the gun." He held out his hand, palm up. "I can slip outside without anyone seeing me and find out what's going on out there."

She lifted her fingers and pressed them against his lips. "Listen...it stopped. I don't hear any more gun shots."

"That doesn't mean someone's not still out there," he pointed out.

His lips moving against her skin had her fingers tingling and her pulse tripping. She was more concerned about who was inside—not out. And while he wasn't exactly in bed with her, he had one knee on the mattress as he leaned over her.

He leaned closer, his gaze intense as he demanded, "Give me the damn gun!"

She almost wished she really had a one. "I can't do that."

"You don't trust me."

"No, I don't," she admitted. "That's why I'm surprised that you didn't grab the gun last night while I was in the shower."

"Knowing you had it helped me avoid temptation," he admitted. His gruff voice and the hot look in his eyes raised goose bumps on her skin.

"Temptation?"

"You." He leaned so close now that he pressed her down into the mattress as his long, lean body covered hers. "Ever since you unzipped that damn body bag, I've been tempted to do this...."

In one hand, he held her neck, his thumb tipping up her chin. And he lowered his head. Slowly. He was giving her time to fight him, to grab for the gun he wanted.

But she had been struggling with temptation, too. Even though she knew she couldn't trust him, she was attracted to him. So attracted that she wanted his kiss no matter his motives for initiating it.

She arched her neck into his hand, lifting her head to close the distance between his mouth and hers. First his breath, escaping in a ragged sigh, caressed her lips. And then his lips brushed across hers in a soft, almost nothing kiss that just teased her with a hint of the passion possible between them.

Her heart stopped beating for nearly a second as she waited for him to increase the pressure, to part her lips and really kiss her.

Instead he jerked back and cursed.

And she laughed.

He clutched at his hand, trying to stem the flow of blood from a fresh wound. "What the hell was that?"

She struggled to sit up, wriggling beneath him. Her

hips pressed against his. Despite being hurt, his body was hard and ready for more than that nothing kiss he'd given her.

He groaned and jumped off the bed, still clutching his hand.

"I lied about the gun," she admitted. She lifted the pillow and retrieved her real weapon: the scalpel she'd grabbed back at the morgue.

"You really don't trust me."

"And with good reason." She grabbed his bleeding hand and examined the wound. He would probably need a couple of stitches. She reached for her suture kit. "You tried to take the gun from me."

"I didn't want to use it on you," he said. "I wanted to use it to protect you."

She pulled out a needle and antiseptic. "I don't need you to protect me."

"No, you don't need me," he heartily agreed.

She lifted her gaze from his hand to his face. "We have an agreement. You're going to help Jed."

He nodded. But she worried that he had no intention of keeping his promise—even after he found out who had betrayed him.

"Rowe—"

Her cell rang. And her heart clutched, as it did every time she got a call, with worry that this would be *the* call, the one telling her that her brother hadn't survived his sentence, that he was dead. Her hand trembling, she reached into her purse, which had been under her pillow with the scalpel, and pulled out her phone.

"It's the morgue," she whispered, dread choking her.

"Are you late for work?" Rowe asked, glancing toward the blind-darkened windows.

She shook her head. "It's my day off." She clicked the button and answered, "Hello."

"Macy," Dr. Bernard said, his voice raspy with weariness. "I need you to come in right away."

Apparently he had discovered her "mistake." Just how much was that error going to cost Macy? Just her job, or her life, too?

HE COULDN'T TRUST MACY KLEYN. The bandage on his hand proved that. She had lied about the gun. What else could she be lying about?

He shouldn't care; it didn't matter. He had clothes now, albeit baggy ones, and a knit hat he'd pulled low over his face. Since riding with her back to the hospital, he had access to transportation and a phone in the crowded parking lot. He'd already scouted out one vehicle with a cell phone sitting in the console and another car that would be easy to hot-wire.

Her van would be easy, too. But when he'd checked for a key hidden in the back wheel well, he'd noticed the scraped rear bumper. Black paint had transferred onto a corner of the chrome.

The coroner's van was black. So was the SUV from Blackwoods Penitentiary that was parked next to the coroner's van. Rowe would have gone closer to inspect the vehicles, but a driver sat behind the wheel of the SUV. The warden was here.

Warden James—not her boss—was the reason that Macy had been called into the morgue. That was why

Rowe couldn't take that phone and vehicle and leave, not when she might be in danger.

He really needed a damn gun. Too bad she'd lied about having one.

Would the warden's driver be armed? Could Rowe get enough of a drop on him to overpower and take his weapon from him? Thinking of Macy in danger had him tempted to try....

MACY BLINKED BACK TEARS, but some trembled on her lashes and spilled onto her cheeks. "I'm so sorry. I have no idea how I screwed up so badly."

"Neither do I," Dr. Bernard murmured, his gaze hard as he stared across his desk at her.

"I—I had no idea I'd sent the wrong body to the crematorium," she insisted, working the tears into her voice now so that it quavered.

Warden James's expression was as severe as her boss's and bone-chillingly cold. He stood behind the coroner's chair, as if too anxious to sit. "I have a daughter, Miss Kleyn, who figured out at a young age how to wrap me around her little finger. But I knew what she was doing, just like I know what you're doing. I let Emily get away with it, but you won't. You're wasting your time and mine with these crocodile tears."

She sniffled, as if fighting back the tears. But he was right; they were just crocodile. She hadn't cried real tears in a long time. Three years to be exact.

"Tell me where the prisoner is!" he demanded, and that jagged vein popped out on his forehead again.

"I told you," she said, letting her voice rise with a hint of hysteria. Maybe she could convince the cynical man that her tears were real. "I sent his body to the crematorium."

"And they already burned him," Dr. Bernard said, repeating the information he had been given when he'd called Elliot a short while ago. "They're faxing a photo of the body they burned."

As if on cue, the machine on the credenza behind the coroner's desk beeped. The warden barely waited before ripping the paper from the all-in-one printer. When he lifted it closer to his face, he cursed.

"It was him?" Macy asked, keeping her voice querulous.

James grunted. "So it seems." But he sounded doubtful.

"Will his family be very upset?" she asked, and found herself wondering about Rowe's family.

How long before they noticed that he hadn't returned from his undercover assignment—if he was actually undercover? He had to be telling the truth, though, because if he were actually an escaped convict, he would have hurt her by now.

He would have used that scalpel on her, stolen her money and her van and been long gone. Maybe some of that was happening right now as she sat here with Dr. Bernard and the warden. Rowe was probably gone. And maybe so was her van.

But she was fine…as long as she could convince the warden she had nothing to do with his disappearance.

"The inmate had no family," James claimed.

But was it a lie, part of Rowe's cover, or the sad truth?

"So is this a very big deal then?" she asked with

feigned hopefulness. "If nobody even cares about this prisoner…?"

"I care," the warden replied. "I care that he might not really be dead, that this all might have been an elaborate plan to escape prison."

She gasped in shock. "But he's dead."

"If that's true, then it's a damn good thing," James said.

"Why?" she asked. She couldn't imagine ever wishing someone dead except maybe the person—whoever that was—who had framed her brother.

"Because he's a very dangerous man," Warden James replied. "He's a cold-blooded killer."

She shivered. Rowe had said he'd been undercover as a drug dealer, not a killer. Which one of these men had lied to her?

"And manipulative," the warden continued. "Anyone who would get involved with him, especially anyone gullible enough to help him, is certain to wind up dead."

"Is he the one who killed the prison doctor?" she asked, testing the warden. If he lied about that, he was probably lying about everything.

"No."

"Then who killed him?" Dr. Bernard asked, his voice cracking with emotion over the loss of his longtime friend.

"We suspect the same man who stabbed the missing prisoner," Warden James replied. "That man had also been wounded in the fight and needed medical attention, so he was alone with Doc."

She gasped. Rowe had wounded Jed? He had never admitted that to her.

"Who's the monster that so ruthlessly beat up Doc?" Dr. Bernard asked.

Warden James turned back to Macy, his beady dark eyes so cold and hard that she shivered despite never taking off her parka. "You know that *monster,* Miss Kleyn. He's your brother."

Macy's heart slammed against her ribs. "Jed?"

Her employer gasped and turned on her. "Your brother did this?"

She shook her head. "No. That's not possible. He wouldn't hurt anyone."

"He's in prison because he murdered two people," the warden said. "One of them was his business partner who was also his fraternity brother. The other person was a young police officer."

"Jed was framed," she insisted.

"He was convicted by a jury of his peers. He's a killer, Miss Kleyn. And since he's convinced you otherwise, it makes me question your judgment," he said. "Could someone else have convinced you of his innocence and enlisted your help?"

She resisted the heat of embarrassment from surging into her face. "Your prisoner was very dead when he arrived here. If the stab wound didn't kill him, then being zipped up in that body bag must have. He was definitely dead."

"You better hope he was, miss," Warden James warned her. "Because if you're in any contact with him, you're in grave danger."

"I'd have to be in the grave to be in contact with

him," she persisted, refusing to be intimidated into backing down or confessing all. It was easier to believe the warden was a cold-blooded killer than Rowe Cusack.

Warden James shook his head in disgust. "For your sake—and your brother's—I hope you're telling the truth."

"Her brother," Dr. Bernard said with disgust, "he will be brought up on charges for Doc's murder, won't he?"

The warden shrugged. "The sheriff has to finish his investigation. He's young and inexperienced and overly cautious. He's not convinced that there's enough evidence to bring to our new district attorney. We all know that damn lawyer's more concerned about his career than justice."

If the warden contributed to his reelection campaign, the D.A. might get interested in carrying out the man's idea of justice. Murder.

"Doc deserves better," his friend said, his eyes wet with grief.

"I'll take care of it," Warden James promised.

Macy shivered, chilled by his not-so-subtle threat against Jed. But giving up Rowe, if he was even still around to give up, wouldn't protect Jed. It would only put him in more danger.

"I'll do the sheriff's job for him since he seems unwilling to do it himself," the warden continued. He squeezed the coroner's shoulder then glared at Macy before leaving the office.

Jed was definitely in trouble. Even if Rowe kept his promise to help him, it would probably be too late to save her brother. Pain and fear clutched her heart, so that it ached. Soon she might be grieving like her boss was grieving for his friend, Doc.

"Macy, I can't express how disappointed I am in you." Dr. Bernard leaned back in his chair and ran his hands over his weary face. "I knew there was more to your story of giving up med school and moving here. I even thought it was because of a guy, because some boyfriend had broken your heart."

"That was part of it," she admitted. Her fiancé had thought she was an idiot for believing and defending Jed. And she had been heartbroken that she'd been stupid enough to actually fall for a guy who hadn't really respected her, let alone loved her.

"Your brother was the biggest part of it," the coroner assumed, "and you didn't tell me anything about him. It makes me wonder what else you're keeping from me, Macy."

She couldn't deny that she had other secrets. But to tell him would only put him in danger, too. Unless he was part of it....

He had been close to the prison doctor. How close was he to the prison warden? Was that why he hadn't requested any authorities to look into all the deaths at Blackwoods?

"I thought you were so smart," he said, shaking his head now in disappointment.

"I'm no fool, Dr. Bernard," she defended herself as she had had to too many times before.

"Then how could you have made the mistake of sending the wrong body to the crematorium?" He shook his head in denial of her claim. "You wouldn't have made a mistake like that."

"I was tired and upset. So were you last night," she reminded him.

He nodded. "So tired that it didn't immediately dawn on me what I saw in the morgue last night."

Too scared to ask, she just waited.

"I saw a bloody bandage."

"It must have fallen off the body when I unzipped the bag," she explained even as she mentally kicked herself for not cleaning up. But there hadn't been time with Dr. Bernard coming back, and Bob, and then the warden and his henchmen...

"Why the needle and sutures, Macy?" he persisted. "Why would you be stitching up the wound on a dead man?"

Coming up with a quick lie, she replied, "Practice. I don't want to lose the skills I learned in my premed labs."

"I didn't hire you so that you could practice on the bodies in my morgue."

"Maybe that's why I made that mistake with the crematorium," she said, as if admitting to one of the secrets he'd accused her of keeping, "because I wanted to cover up my handiwork."

"I'm worried that you're covering up more than a few stitches," her employer said. "I can't trust you. You've already been keeping too much from me. I have to let you go."

"Dr. Bernard," she said, protesting her firing. "I worked for you for three years, and this is my first mistake. Please give me another chance."

There were few employment opportunities in Black-woods unless one wanted to work at the prison, and even openings there were rare. People—employees and inmates—only left Blackwoods Penitentiary in body bags.

"I can't do that, Macy," Dr. Bernard said. "I can't trust you. I don't know if you've ever really told me the truth about anything."

She sucked in a breath at the harsh accusation. Until her brother's trial, she had never kept anything from anyone. But she'd learned then that the world wasn't really the place she'd believed it was and that she had to protect herself. "Sir—"

"For your sake, I hope you're not lying about this prisoner," he said. "Because if you helped him escape, you're in danger—not just from him but from Warden James, too. No one crosses that man and lives."

Oh, God, Jed...

"You know the warden's a killer but you haven't done anything about it?" she asked, as horrified and disappointed in him as he seemed to be in her.

His face flushed, mottled with either embarrassment or anger. "You're a naive girl, Macy. You have no idea what the real world is like."

She chuckled bitterly. "I know exactly what the real world is like." Regrettably. "And I don't like it. I don't like it that people stand by and do nothing—"

"And some people get involved when they shouldn't," he interrupted. "And they get hurt. Or worse."

"You're scared of the warden?" She almost hoped that was the only reason he hadn't gotten involved. Fear was better than complicity.

"You should be scared of Warden James, too," the coroner warned her. "If he finds out that you helped this inmate escape…" He shuddered, as if he was imagining all the horrible things that he would discover had been done to her when he examined her dead body in his morgue.

"There's nothing for him to find out," she said, refusing to drop her bluff even though those knots of fear tightened in her stomach.

"I don't believe you," he said. "And neither did Warden James."

No. She doubted that he had, too. But he had no proof that she was lying until he found Rowe. He couldn't find Rowe. Hopefully the man, whatever he really was, was long gone.

"The warden is paranoid," she said. "That corpse didn't walk out of here."

The older man nodded in agreement. "No. He had help getting out of here. He had you."

She couldn't keep lying to a man she had once respected, so she just shook her head.

"Like you, this prisoner can't be trusted either," Dr. Bernard said. "Whatever he told you to enlist your aid could be just as many lies as you've told me."

"Dr. Bernard—"

"Just clear out all of your things and leave," her boss said, covering his eyes as if unable to look at her anymore. "I don't want to see you again."

Tears—real tears—stung her eyes, and she blinked them back. "I'm sorry…"

"I don't want to see you in my morgue either," he

added. "I don't want to unzip a body bag and find you inside it, Macy."

"You won't—"

"I will. It's inevitable," he said with a fatalistic sigh, "because you have put your trust in the wrong people. You're a smart girl, Macy. Start using your head before you wind up losing your life."

Maybe he was right. Maybe she shouldn't have trusted Rowe Cusack; that might not even be his real name. She had only his word for who he really was. She had only his word that he wasn't the dangerous, murderous convict the warden claimed he was.

And if the warden was right, there was a very good chance that Macy would wind up back in the morgue— in that body bag, just as Dr. Bernard feared.

Chapter Six

Rowe had been right to trust her to handle the meeting on her own. Not that he would have been able to accompany her, since his presence would have only put her in more danger. And he didn't know of anyone he could have trusted to go along with her to the meeting either. But he had also doubted that her boss would have let the warden hurt her. As it had played out, though, Dr. Bernard had been the one who'd hurt her.

"The coroner fired you?" he asked, as she settled her box of belongings onto the passenger's seat beside her. Once again, he was crouched down in the back of the van.

She shrugged as if it didn't matter, but pain darkened her brown eyes to nearly black when she glanced back at him. "I expected consequences for what I did last night. I knew I would get in trouble for helping you."

"But you still helped me." He didn't know anyone else who would have.

"I only helped you for Jed," she clarified, as if she was worried that he would misconstrue her involvement with him. After the kiss, he didn't blame her for worrying. That kiss worried him, too. "I have to protect

Jed and get you to help him. Can you even help him, though?"

"I won't know for sure until I get a chance to go over all of the evidence the prosecutor had against him," he admitted. And he suspected it must have been substantial for a jury to have convicted him.

She gave an eager nod. "We can get the files from his lawyer."

"Not yet," Rowe reminded her. "I can't do anything as a dead man, or as an escaped convict. First, I have to find out who blew my cover to the warden."

She reached into the box in the passenger's seat, pulled out a cell phone and handed it back to him. "So find out."

"I can't use your phone," he protested, keeping his hand at his side. "The call can be traced back to you."

"This call will be traced back to Mr. Mortimer. I took the cell from his personal effects." She thrust the phone at him until he finally closed his fingers around it.

He had no idea who to call. No idea who to trust.

She must have sensed his hesitation because she said, "There must be someone who can help you."

"You've worked so hard to prove me dead," he pointed out. "With one call, I can undo all your work once someone hears and recognizes my voice."

"True." She took the phone back. "So I'll make the call. What's the number?"

His head pounded with frustration for his inability to do anything for himself right now without risking her life and his. "What number?"

"For the DEA," she replied matter-of-factly.

Dr. Bernard hadn't just hurt her. He and the warden had unnerved her. Whatever they'd said to her had brought back all her doubts about him. Gone was the woman who had teased and kissed him just hours ago.

So he gave her the direct number to his office and watched her face as she listened to his message. "That extension is no longer working," she informed him.

"That's my direct line." And the call should have gone to his voice mail. Even though he spent most of his time in the field, he still had an office in the Drug Enforcement Administration building in Detroit.

Maybe word had gotten back to the administration about his "death." He grabbed the phone from her and punched in another number for the department secretary. He handed the phone back to her while it rang.

"Hello," she said. "I'd like to speak to someone about Agent Rowe Cusack." She listened for a moment then clicked off the cell.

"Nobody would talk to you about me," he surmised.

"No." She closed her eyes and shook her head. "Because nobody knows who you are."

"I'm deep undercover," he reminded her. "It's protocol not to risk it."

"Your cover's been blown," she said. "As far as they know, you're dead. Why deny you exist?"

Why? He damn well wondered himself. "You could be anyone calling. A reporter. My killer."

"Who are you?" she asked, her dark eyes narrowed with suspicion as she stared back at him. "Really. Who are you?"

"I told you."

"And I was a fool to believe your story just because you know about some old scar on my head."

He suspected that she had more scars than the one on her head. She had some on her heart, too. He wasn't the only one who had been betrayed and now struggled to trust anyone.

"What happened in there?" he asked, the concern that had tortured him during her meeting rushed back over him, quickening his pulse. He reached between the seats and tried to grasp her hand.

But she shrank away from him, as if afraid or repulsed.

She hadn't acted repulsed just a short time ago when he'd covered her body with his and kissed her lips. In fact she had seemed to want more. More of a kiss. More than a kiss…

He had wanted more, too. That brief taste of her sweet lips had made him hungry for her. He'd wanted to take her mouth and then her sweet body. But he had already used her enough.

"Are you all right?" he asked, worried that the warden had hurt or had threatened her.

She shook her head again. But her face was deathly pale, as if she'd suddenly gotten sick. "No. I think I made a terrible mistake."

"I haven't lied to you, Macy." But he suspected she was lying, at least by omission. Something else had happened besides her being fired.

"You won't be able to help Jed," she said with a weary sigh of resignation, as if she'd already accepted that he wasn't going to keep his promise. "You don't even know how to help yourself."

"I know how," he insisted, pride smarting. "I have a plan."

He had to go to Detroit, to the office, and confront all of his possible betrayers. Only a few people knew the details of his undercover assignment. "But I'm worried about you."

His promise to Jed, to keep her safe, had become the most important of all the promises he had ever made. Not that he'd made many; he knew better than to make promises he might not be able to keep given the danger of his profession.

"Haven't I proved that I can take care of myself?" she asked. "I don't need you. And you don't need me. You have your plan."

"What do you have?" he wondered. "You just lost your job." And maybe her brother. Since the warden was convinced that Rowe wasn't dead, he must know that Jed had disobeyed his order to kill. The egomaniacal control freak would not tolerate disobedience.

She shrugged again, as if it didn't matter to her that she had nothing anymore. But he knew better. "Right now, I just want some space," she insisted. "Some time to think."

"You want me gone." He didn't blame her. Since turning up in the morgue in that body bag, he had turned her life upside down.

She didn't deny that she wanted him to go away. "You can go to the sheriff," she suggested. "The warden doesn't own him. Yet."

"How do you know that?"

She lifted her arms, extending her wrists beyond the

sleeves of her jacket. "He hasn't slapped the cuffs on me yet."

"The warden wanted you arrested?"

"The warden wants you," she said. "And he'll use whatever and whoever he needs to in order to get you."

"So Doc must have given up that I'm not dead." He couldn't blame him either. The old man had taken a beating. He probably would have given up his own mother to stop the pain.

Damn it. Then Macy Kleyn's brother was probably already dead.

She sighed. "I don't know. Warden James suspects you're alive, but he doesn't know for sure, especially since your body's gone missing."

He chuckled in remembrance of exactly how his body went missing. "You bought me some time with your ruse at the crematorium."

She nodded. "So stop wasting that time."

She reached into the box and lifted out a ring of keys. "Take this and get the hell out of Blackwoods County."

He studied the keys; one was clearly for an ignition. "There was a car in someone's personal effects, too?"

"It's mine."

"But you have this van…." And he doubted she made enough even at both of her jobs to afford payments, license and insurance on two vehicles.

"This van is Elliot's," she explained. "He bought it and put it in my name, so that his dad wouldn't know he uses it for gigs. We switch, and I drive the hearse to the crematorium on the nights his band plays."

She and this Elliot were close. She had friends in

Blackwoods, people she could trust. He didn't have to worry about her. He took the car keys from her hand but closed his fingers around hers.

"I'm sorry," he said. "If there had been any other way, I wouldn't have gotten your brother and you involved in this."

"I just wish I knew, without a doubt, what *this* was," she said wistfully, and then she shook her head. "It doesn't matter, though. Goodbye."

He wanted to kiss her. But he just squeezed her fingers once before releasing her. Then he opened the sliding side door and slipped out of the van. And out of her life. Despite his promise to her brother, it was the right thing to do. She would be safer without him in it.

HE THOUGHT HER BROTHER was dead; she had seen the regret in his blue eyes when he'd squeezed her hand. Rowe believed it was too late for Jed.

Macy couldn't believe it until she saw for herself that her brother was really gone. So the minute the door slid closed behind the man whose body bag she'd unzipped less than twenty-four hours ago, she started the van and headed toward the prison on the heavily wooded outskirts of Blackwoods County.

Even during the day the winding roads were treacherous, but in her emotional state with her heart pumping slowly and heavily with dread and with tears of grief filling her eyes, Macy struggled to keep the van in her lane.

If she crossed the solid yellow lines, she could be struck by another vehicle coming fast around a sharp curve. Or if she went off the shoulder, she could roll the van into one of the deep ditches. Usually those ditches were filled with water that had drowned more than one hapless driver in the three years she had been working at Blackwoods County morgue.

Despite her emotional state, she wasn't hapless. But the driver behind her was. Just like the night before, the vehicle came up fast and struck her rear bumper. But the impact was harder, so hard that the van spun out. Macy gripped the wheel hard, fighting to keep it from the ditch. And the only way to do that was to go across that yellow line.

With a sharp curve ahead she couldn't see what was coming up. Logging trucks frequented these northern Michigan roads. And with the weight of their loads, they were unable to stop quickly. She stomped on the brakes, her tires squealing.

She had avoided the ditch on her right, but a horn blew as the van careened around the corner, straight into the path of an oncoming car. The sedan's tires squealed as it swerved around her.

But Macy couldn't breathe yet or let go of the wheel, because now the van slid toward the ditch on the left. But the gravel shoulder widened for a scenic turn-out overlooking a steep ravine. She managed to steer the van for that wider stretch of gravel and stop at the pylons that separated the shoulder from the tree-filled ravine below.

Finally she released the cry of terror she had been holding inside. But her relief was short-lived. The van creaked as someone yanked open her driver's door. She caught only a glimpse of a tall, dark shadow as strong hands grabbed at her shoulder, pulling her from the van.

She kicked out and clawed with her hands, fighting for her life. But her attacker was undeterred, his foot only slipping a bit on the gravel as he wrapped his arms around her from behind.

She reached back into the van, managing to grab the strap of her purse and drag it with her as he lifted her off her feet. She tried to twist around, trying to see his face, trying to fight.

But he was too strong, his arms wound too tightly around her for her to wriggle free. He carried her toward the black SUV he had left running behind the van, blocking the road. When he let go of her with one arm to open the back door, Macy wrenched loose from his grasp.

She ran, and as she ran, she reached inside her purse for the weapon she'd stashed inside, the one that had already wounded one man. But before her fingers could close around the scalpel, a hand grasped her hair, jerking her ponytail with such force that tears trickled from the corners of her eyes.

Another strong hand, on her arm, swung her around. But before she could focus on the face of her attacker, a fist came toward her, catching her off guard.

She couldn't duck. She could do nothing to avoid the blow. Pain exploded in her face, staggering her so that her legs gave way, folding beneath her.

And as she fell to the ground, her vision blurred, blackness overwhelming her as she lost consciousness and the fight for her life.

INSTINCTS—THE SAME ONES that had warned him that his cover had been blown—had compelled Rowe to follow

Macy instead of the signs that would have led him out
of Blackwoods County. When he'd noticed the black
SUV also following her, Rowe had known he was right
to trust the instincts that had clenched his stomach muscles into tight knots of dread.

But he didn't know the back roads as well as Macy
and her stalker, so he couldn't drive as fast and he
lost sight of them around the hairpin turns. While he
couldn't anticipate the sharp curves, he recognized the
road as the one that would lead him straight back to
hell.

Blackwoods Penitentiary.

He should have known she was going to check on
her brother. If the warden had discovered her relation-
ship to Blackwoods' notorious inmate, he would have
exploited it for her cooperation. James had probably
threatened Jed's life.

But instead of giving up Rowe to save her brother,
Macy had given up herself if she was going to Blackwoods. Just because she was visiting didn't mean she
couldn't be held at the prison until she told the warden
what he wanted to know. Since the heartless bastard
had had no problem beating an old man to death, he
would have no problem torturing Macy into telling him
everything. Except that Macy was stubborn and loyal
and smart. She would die before she gave up any information that would put her brother in danger.

The next curve brought Rowe around to her van,
where it was parked precariously on the shoulder of
the wrong side of the road. The rear bumper wasn't
just dented now but smashed up into the back quarter
panels.

With his heart hammering, he pulled up behind the van and vaulted out of the car Macy had loaned him. Had she been driving that instead, whatever vehicle had struck her would have pushed her right over the edge into the ravine. As he rushed around to the driver's side of her borrowed van, he nearly slipped in the loose gravel and fell off the road into the ravine below. Hell, she'd nearly gone over in the van.

The woman was a damn good driver. Another few inches, and she would have snapped the pylons and rolled down into the ravine that was so steep and heavily wooded that the van might have never been found. And since she would have surely been hurt in the crash, Macy wouldn't have been able to get help. She could have lain down there, suffering. Or dead and undiscovered.

The driver's door of the van gaped open, the interior empty of everything but that sad cardboard box of her work belongings. If Macy had gotten out of the vehicle of her own accord, she would still be on the road. He hadn't been that far behind her that he wouldn't see her now as he stood on the wide turnout and stared in both directions. Even if she was running through the woods or the ravine, whoever had run her off the road would be chasing her, their vehicle left behind.

But there were no other vehicles besides the van and her car here. Whatever had run her off the road was gone, and so was Macy.

She wouldn't have gone without a fight. So whoever had taken her had been strong enough or armed enough to overpower her. He stared down at the gravel shoulder. It was loose and scattered onto the asphalt lane of the road. Maybe the tires had kicked up the gravel. Or maybe Macy's kicking feet had.

Then he noticed something else on the pavement. Droplets of blood, like cast-off, from a wound.

"Dear God…" He closed his eyes on the image in his mind, of her bleeding and in pain. He had to help her and not just because of that promise he'd made her brother.

He ran back to her car and slid behind the wheel again. He had to find her before she wound up like Doc, tortured and dead.

Because of him…

"You have her?" His phone clutched to his ear, Warden James settled into his office chair with a sigh of relief. "You took her where I told you to?"

Where no one would be able to hear her screams…

There would be no more fake tears from Macy Kleyn. He would make her cry for real. And he would make her tell him the damn truth. All of it. Like what the hell she'd really done with that damn DEA agent…

"Yes," his flunky replied with pride. "She's unconscious now but starting to come around."

James was actually surprised the guy had pulled it off. Macy Kleyn was more resourceful than he would have expected a girl who wasn't much older than his own daughter to be. Emily was smart, smarter than most people realized. But she was also sweet and softhearted and incredibly naive because he had always sheltered her from the real world. She couldn't find out the truth about him and all the things he'd done.

He would do anything to protect her from the truth of that—even kill again. And again.

"Good," James said, "I will be there shortly." While he'd had his guard work over Doc, he wanted to deal with Miss Kleyn personally. He could use her for more than just information on the whereabouts of the missing DEA officer.

But a knock sounded at his door. Without waiting for James to grant admission, his head guard opened the door. "Warden, the situation is getting worse. We need to call the sheriff."

James snorted. "York? You think that kid could handle a situation like this? He'd get himself killed." So maybe it wouldn't be such a bad thing to call him.

"You're right," the correction officer agreed. "This is too much for the sheriff's office. Hell, we may need to call in the National Guard."

"Not yet," James snapped. "And make sure the alarms are still disarmed." It was *his* damn prison; he would regain control of it on his own. He already had a plan for that.

"Warden?" The question came from the man on the phone James had forgotten he still held. "Is everything all right?"

No. It hadn't been all right since the day Rowe Cusack had set foot in Blackwoods. If only James's damn partner could have stopped the DEA from investigating.

"You should get started without me," he said, with another sigh, this one of resignation. James glanced out the window toward the cement wall and barbed wire fence. The prison was still contained. "I have to deal with a situation here."

And having Macy Kleyn would make dealing with that "situation" a whole lot easier. Now he had leverage supporting his threats.

But he still needed one more thing. Rowe Cusack. "Get her to talk. Get her to tell you where that damn federal agent is hiding."

"Warden," the head guard called for his attention again. "We've got to do something to get control."

"We will," James maintained. "It's just a matter of time." However long it took to break the girl…

She wouldn't be as brave or stubborn as Doc had been. She wouldn't be able to hold out long.

"We don't have much time," the guard warned him. "There have already been a couple of casualties. On both sides."

A prisoner and a guard.

Before the day was over, James anticipated a couple more casualties.

Macy Kleyn and Rowe Cusack.

Chapter Seven

A throbbing in her jaw dragged Macy from the sweet oblivion of unconsciousness. She opened her eyes and blinked against the bright sunshine pouring through a high window in what appeared to be a plywood wall.

Where was she?

Damn it! Damn it all to hell that she'd passed out. Now she had no idea where she was or how long it had taken to drive there. Once she got loose, she wouldn't know where to run. But getting loose might be a problem.

She wriggled but her hands were bound behind her, rope scraping the skin on her wrists. Pain radiated up her arms, echoing that dull ache in her jaw. And her neck was strained, hurt from hanging at an odd angle. She'd been tied to a straight-back chair; her ankles bound like her wrists and tethered to the chair legs.

Squinting against the light, she peered around the room. One quick glance confirmed that she was alone. For now. With pine board walls and floor, it was a cabin, one room like the one she rented, but this space was much smaller. There was no kitchen or bath. Hell, it might have been just a shed. Something scurried in the shadows near the baseboards, little feet scraping over the leather of her purse. It was just an arm's length away, but she couldn't reach it.

She couldn't save herself. And she had sent away the one man who could have helped her. Why had she let the warden and Dr. Bernard make her doubt herself? Make her doubt Jed?

Her brother wouldn't have told Rowe about that accident in her childhood if he hadn't wanted to send her the message to trust the man he'd sent to her in a body bag.

It didn't matter that the Drug Enforcement Administration had denied Rowe Cusack. Hell, that only proved more that he was telling the truth, that someone in his own agency had betrayed him. And he had gone off alone to track down his betrayer. She suspected he might wind up as she was about to—dead.

Unless she figured out how to get free…

She strained her sore arms, tugging at the ropes again, but the fibers bit into her skin, too tight to give her even a little wiggle room. She could not get her hands loose. She could not get loose.

When the door swung open and her attacker stepped inside, she vowed to herself that she wouldn't betray Rowe, too, no matter what this man did to her. She might not be able to save herself but she wouldn't be the reason that harm came to Rowe or her brother.

"Where is he?" he asked.

The guy was tall but so skinny that she wondered how he had managed to strike her with such force. His dark hair was long and stringy, hanging well past his thin shoulders. He looked young and vaguely familiar.

Where had she seen him before?

"Where is he?" he asked again, stepping closer. He struck her again, this time with an open hand instead of a closed fist.

Her skin stung from the slap. "Who?"

"You know who—Rowe Cusack."

Her blood chilled. This guy, whoever he was, wasn't even bothering with using Rowe's undercover identity. He knew who Rowe was. Why hadn't anyone in the DEA admitted to knowing him?

But now she found herself denying him. "I don't know who that is."

"That's the guy you helped escape from Blackwoods prison," the kid informed her, as if she would have helped Rowe had she not at least known his name.

She may have doubted him with her head. But deep inside, she'd believed he was really a lawman.

She shook her head. "I didn't help anyone escape. I haven't even been up to the prison."

In a week. It had been a week since she had seen her brother. If only she'd known then that it might have been her last time....

Instead of being a smart-ass and teasing him, she would have been serious. She would have told him how much she appreciated his being her white knight while they were growing up. She would have told him how much she loved him.

"No," the guy agreed, "your job was to get Cusack out of the morgue."

How could this man know that? Unless Jed...

What had they done to her brother to get him to give her up? But nothing could have compelled him. Jed would have gone to his grave before he uttered her name. But yet he had mentioned her…to Rowe. Her brother would have only done that if he'd truly trusted that Rowe wouldn't have hurt her.

Why hadn't she trusted him?

"I work at the morgue. I assist Dr. Bernard," she said.

The skinny guy shuddered at the mention of the morgue. How could someone be creeped out by death but have no problem with killing? If he'd forced her off into the ravine, she would have died.

"Assist?" She laughed at herself. "I just clean up after the coroner and do some of his paperwork. That's all I do."

"You helped the prisoner last night."

Was he talking about the sutures? She hadn't thought Dr. Bernard had told anyone about her suturing Rowe's wound.

"It was too late for that inmate," she insisted. "He was already dead when he showed up at the morgue yesterday."

"We need proof of that."

"We?" she asked. "Who are you working for? Warden James?" Or whoever had given up Rowe in the DEA? How deep did this corruption run?

The man slapped her again, so hard that the chair teetered and tipped over, knocking her onto the floor. Her shoulder burned, from her arms being bound and from the force with which she hit the boards. But that pain was the least of her worries when the man kicked out and struck her stomach with the hard toe of his work boot.

The breath left her lungs, and a scream slipped

through her lips. She gathered enough breath and screamed again, so loud that it echoed in the room and throughout her own skull.

The skeevy guy laughed. "Scream all you want. Nobody will hear you out here, Macy Kleyn. I can do whatever I want to you and nobody will know."

She shivered at the lascivious look that crossed his gaunt face as he stared down at her. Then she glanced toward her purse. She had fallen away from it. But even if she could reach it now, she would never be able to get the scalpel out of it in time to defend herself.

"I have proof!" she insisted. "They take pictures at the crematorium, of the bodies they burn. His picture was there. Dr. Bernard has a faxed copy of it."

"That doesn't prove the guy was really dead when that picture was taken. Anybody can play dead, and I guess this Rowe character is really good at it," he said. "That picture only proves that you brought him to the crematorium."

How did he know *she* had brought him? She'd told the warden that the crematorium was picking up the body. This guy must have followed her from the hospital last night. The warden must have doubted her story from the very beginning and left someone behind to tail her.

"He's dead!" she yelled as the guy reached for her. She couldn't even kick out, not with her legs bound to the chair. But then his hands were there, untying her ankles as he pulled her closer.

"If he's not dead," the man said, as he slid his hands up her legs to her waist and fumbled with the snap of her jeans, "then by the time I'm through with you, you're going to wish he was."

"No, you're the one who's going to wish I was really dead," a deep voice murmured.

THE MAN AND MACY BOTH TURNED toward the open door. It hadn't even been locked. But it wouldn't have mattered if it had been. When he'd heard her scream, Rowe would have kicked it down to get to her.

His heart pounded hard, as hard as he wanted to pound the guy who had his filthy hands on her. The weasel had already hurt her, because her face was red and swelling. A small cut on her cheek must have been the source of the blood droplets that had fallen onto the asphalt.

"Get away from her!" he shouted.

A grin spread across the man's face. "This is great. I'll be able to give James the proof that you're finally dead when I hand over your body myself." He reached behind his back, but he was so skinny that Rowe could see what he reached for—the gun he had tucked into the waistband of his jeans.

Macy screamed again and kicked her legs at the man with such force that she knocked him to the ground. But he didn't drop the gun.

Instead he swung the barrel toward her and snarled, "You bitch!"

Rowe grabbed for the gun just as it went off. The guy's grip was tight on the gun and on the trigger. Shot after shot fired. Rowe couldn't take the risk that a bullet wouldn't hit her. If one hadn't already…

So he wrapped his arm around the guy's neck. And with one quick twist and crunch of bones, he snapped it.

Macy gasped, her dark eyes wide with shock, as wide and shocked as the eyes of her dead attacker.

She had doubted and feared Rowe before. What he'd just had to do—kill a man with his bare hands right in front of her—would only scare her more.

"Are you all right?" he asked.

Her eyes still wide, she only nodded.

He expected her to shrink back when he reached for the bindings at her wrists, but she only stared up at him as he tugged at the knot.

"Grab my purse," she suggested when the knot refused to budge. "The scalpel's inside it."

A grin tugged at his lips. "Of course it is." Using his already bandaged hand, he carefully reached inside the leather bag.

"It's in my wallet."

He pulled out the metal handle and sliced the blade neatly through the thick rope. His hand throbbed in remembrance of how sharp her damn weapon was.

If only she'd managed to get hold of it before the man had grabbed her… Then it would have been his blood spattered on the asphalt.

He skimmed his fingertips gently along her swollen jaw and over the short cut. Blood smeared her silky skin. "He hit you."

And knowing that the man had hurt her expunged whatever regrets Rowe had about having to kill him. Sure, it would have been better to take him alive and find out who had sent him after Macy.

But Rowe was already pretty certain who had done

that. The guy didn't look familiar to him, though. With his long, scraggly hair, he hadn't been one of the brush-cut prison guards, who were on the warden's payroll.

So who was this man who'd grabbed and intended to assault Macy?

Her thick lashes fluttered as if she were fighting back tears. "I'm okay."

He gently probed the bruise, tracing the delicate bone beneath her skin. "Are you sure your jaw's not dislocated?"

She shook her head, dislodging his hand from her face so that his fingers skimmed down her throat. Her breath audibly caught.

With fear? Now, after seeing him kill her kidnapper, she knew exactly how violent he could be.

She leaned closer and took her weapon from him. She slid it back into her wallet and her wallet into her purse.

"I'm fine," she stubbornly insisted, even though her entire body trembled now as if in reaction to her ordeal.

What had happened was bad enough. What could have happened even worse.

No wonder she was shaking. They needed to get the hell out of the cabin, because this guy had definitely not been acting alone. He was working for someone who could show up at any time. But he couldn't move her until she got over her initial shock.

"You're not fine," Rowe argued. He wished he could close his arms around her and offer her comfort. But she didn't trust him so his holding her would only upset her more.

But then her arms slid around his neck and she

pressed her body against his as she clutched him tightly. "I'm fine…because of you."

He resisted the urge, barely, to press her even more tightly against him so that he could feel her every heartbeat and assure himself she was really all right. When he'd heard her scream with such pain and fear, he'd thought he was too late, that he wouldn't be able to save her.

Emotion choking him, he could only utter her name, "Macy…"

She eased back in his loose embrace and smiled up at him. "Thank you for coming back."

"I didn't really leave."

"Why not?" She pulled completely out of his arms, her brow furrowing in confusion. "You had my car and that phone…."

But he hadn't had her. Not that he needed her. He just had to assure himself that she was safe. He'd made a promise to Jed. A promise he intended to keep.

"It's good I had the car," he said. "I was able to follow you."

"You were behind me?"

"Until you lost me." She was a better driver than the man who'd run her off the road.

Rowe had caught up to the black SUV just as it had slowed for the turnoff to the two-track road that had led through the woods to this small cabin. Since the car didn't have four-wheel drive like the SUV, he hadn't even been able to take it all the way down the nearly washed out driveway. But walking up to the cabin had given him the element of surprise, even if it had put Macy in more danger.

And through more pain.

"I'm glad you found me," she said.

"Me, too."

She glanced down at the dead man and shuddered. "He was going to…"

Torture her, even more violently than Doc had been tortured.

"You could have just told him the truth," he said. But she hadn't. Of course, she wouldn't have been giving up just him—she would have been giving up her brother, too.

"I don't think it matters," she said. "My plan didn't work. They're convinced you're alive."

"Doc must have talked before he died." If only he and Jed hadn't had to involve the prison doctor. But they'd had few options…besides Rowe really dying. "Were you on your way to Blackwoods when this guy ran you off the road?"

She nodded. "I wanted to see Jed."

"You need to stay away from there." He touched the bruise on her face again, skimming his fingertips gently across the swollen skin. "You have to get the hell out of Blackwoods."

There was nothing left for her in this county any longer. She'd lost her job. And Rowe suspected that she'd lost her reason for moving here in the first place. She'd lost her brother.

If Doc had admitted that Rowe was alive, then Jed was already dead.

"Come with me," he urged, leaning closer to her. Close enough that he could almost taste her breath again.

She tilted her head, her messy ponytail swishing over her shoulder. "Do you hear that?"

A motor revved as a vehicle headed down the driveway toward the cabin.

"We need to get going," he said, helping her to her feet as he stood up himself. Her legs didn't fold beneath her; she was already over her slight bout of shock.

The woman impressed the hell out of him. But then she stubbornly shook her head. "We can't leave yet," she said.

"You're right." He reached down and grabbed the gun from the dead man's hand. From now on, Rowe would be armed. When he tugged on her hand to pull her toward the door, she planted her feet and resisted.

"We have to hide the body," she insisted.

"There's no time." The engine noise grew louder as the vehicle closed in on the cabin.

"If someone finds him like this, they'll have their proof that you're alive. They'll know that there's no way I—" her breath caught "—could have broken his neck."

"You know that I had no choice."

Her head jerked in a nod. "He had the gun. And I think he was high on something. He was superhumanly strong."

So if he hadn't been one of the warden's employees at the prison, he had been one of his customers. And loyal or indebted enough to willingly do the warden's dirty work for him.

"You had no choice," she said, exonerating him of any guilt over the killing.

"And we have no choice now," he said. "We have to get out of here." He reached for the dead man again, but for his keys this time. If they had any chance of outrunning whoever was coming, they would have to take his SUV and leave Macy's car.

"Sounds echo in the woods," she said. "Like those gunshots you heard this morning."

The shots had awakened him from a sound sleep and dreams about her. But the dream hadn't compared to the reality of her body beneath his, of her breath teasing his lips as he'd lowered his head.

"That vehicle could be a ways off," she assured him.

Or it could be driving up right behind the dead man's SUV, trapping them at the cabin.

Her abductor had fired off most of the shots in the magazine. If Rowe couldn't find more ammunition, the weapon was useless. And if there was more than one person in the vehicle approaching the cabin, he might not be able to fight off all of them.

Chapter Eight

"Son of a bitch!" James slammed the door of the small, *empty* shed.

But before he headed back to the SUV and his waiting driver, he reached for the untraceable cell and punched in that damn speed dial number he had begun to dread calling.

"Tell me Cusack is dead," was the greeting with which the phone was answered.

"I can't," James said, his head pounding with frustration and stress.

"What the hell do you mean?" was the incredulous question. "You can't track down his damn body?"

"I thought I had a lead on him." He glanced back to the empty cabin. Had the kid really had her or had he, like so many other people had lately, lied to James? "But she's gone."

"She?"

"There's a young woman who may have helped him escape." And she was just as resourceful and resilient as James had worried she was. She was too much like her damn brother. That was another reason the warden needed to get a hold of that girl.

A snort rattled the phone. "Given what Rowe Cusack

looks like, it makes sense that a *woman* would have helped him. Usually Cusack's all business though. He doesn't get involved with anyone on the job, or as far as I know, *off* it either. He's always been a real loner. I can't imagine him partnering up with anyone."

But then James's partner hadn't seen the girl. She was as pretty as she was deceitful.

"I've had my men search everywhere for him." The morgue. The crematorium. Her cabin. He really hadn't had the manpower to spare for a thorough search, though; that was why he'd enlisted that damn kid.

"You're going to have to search harder," his partner said, stating the obvious.

"If he's as good as you think he is, then he really is alive and as far from Blackwoods County—" and the warden's reach "—as he can get." And even though there would be repercussions for James if the man was alive, he would be happy as hell if Rowe Cusack was out of his jurisdiction.

"Cusack isn't going to just go into hiding and let you get away with trying to have him killed."

James sighed. "No, he won't. But he'll also know there's no one in Blackwoods that he can trust." Except for that damn girl. "And he'll want to find out who in the DEA blew his cover." He hadn't had many dealings with Cusack, but the warden understood wanting to know who had betrayed him. And getting vengeance for that betrayal…

Another gasp whistled through the phone. "So you think he's on his way here?"

"Don't you?"

Curses rattled the phone.

"Cusack's your problem now," James said, with relief, before breaking the connection. He had big enough troubles of his own.

"I'M SURPRISED YOU'RE NOT gloating," Rowe remarked with a glance over at Macy in the passenger seat of her small coupe.

Jed had bought her the car when she'd graduated premed with an MCAT score that would have had med schools fighting over her had she had time to apply before he'd been arrested. She had given up so much for him, but she had a horrible feeling that he had given up more for her.

His life. He would have died before he'd told the warden anything that would have caused his little sister harm.

If only Macy could have asked Rowe to go to the prison, so that she would know for certain if her brother lived or if he was already gone....

But then she would have been asking Rowe to give up his life, too. Instead he was trying to take it back, driving southeast to Detroit and the field office of the Drug Enforcement Administration from which he worked.

"What?" she asked, not following his remark. "Why would I be gloating?"

"You were right about that vehicle we heard. It was farther off than it sounded," he explained. "Hell, it hadn't even been coming from the road."

The noise had been coming from farther down the two-track, which Macy suspected led to a back entrance to Blackwoods Penitentiary.

"Do you think we hid his body well enough to buy ourselves—" and Jed "—some time?"

"Putting him in the SUV and sending it down into that ravine was genius," he praised her.

"Then when he is found—" and that could take quite a while in Blackwoods County "—Dr. Bernard will think his neck was broken in the crash since he wasn't belted into the vehicle."

"Just wish we knew who he was…" And why he had looked vaguely familiar to her.

"The vehicle was registered to the prison." The registration was all they had found inside the glove box. The guy hadn't had his wallet on him, so they hadn't found his driver's license.

"But he was no guard," Rowe insisted, "not looking like that."

"And not with his being on drugs," Macy agreed.

Rowe snorted. "A drug addiction wouldn't disqualify him from being a guard at Blackwoods."

"They're users?"

"And dealers."

"You learned a lot during the little while you were undercover," she said. He really was good at his job; he hadn't been just bragging when he'd told her he was.

"I learned enough to get myself killed." He sighed. "But nobody tries all that hard to hide anything at Blackwoods. They're not very worried about getting caught."

"It's like they think they're above the law?"

"Or they've just bought it off," he bitterly remarked.

She suspected that Rowe wasn't only talking about the sheriff of Blackwoods County. The former one had definitely been on the warden's payroll. And if the new sheriff wasn't yet, he probably would be soon. As Dr. Bernard had proved, everyone in Blackwoods was aware of how dangerous and corrupt the warden was but yet no one did anything to stop him.

Until now. Until Rowe Cusack.

A muscle twitched along his jaw as the freeway widened to several lanes. They were nearing the city and his betrayer, which was whoever the warden had bought off inside the Drug Enforcement Administration.

"Didn't anyone try to bribe you while you were inside?" she wondered.

He snorted again. "It would have been easier to kill me than pay me. I was a sitting duck in prison."

Like Jed was now.

"I'm sorry," he said, as if he had read her mind and had known that she would immediately think of her brother.

"You're not the one who put Jed in there." She forced a smile to assure him that she was all right. She wasn't about to dissolve into hysterical sobs. Crying wouldn't help either Rowe or Jed, if it was still possible for her brother to be helped.

"I'll find out who did," he promised.

Even if her brother was already dead? But even posthumously Jed would appreciate having his name cleared. So would she.

"First you need to find out who betrayed you." She had to focus on that now. She could still help Rowe. "What's your plan?"

He shrugged, his broad shoulders rippling beneath the thin knit shirt of her brother's he'd borrowed. "It probably has to be my handler." A muscle twitched along his tightly clenched jaw, as if that betrayal was hard for him to accept.

"You don't want to believe it's him?"

"No. We've worked together for years. I trusted Donald Jackson. I thought we both cared..." His throat moved as he swallowed hard. "But it has to be him. Or it doesn't make sense that he didn't pull me out when I was denied privileges and didn't contact him."

"But you think it could go higher than your handler?" she realized.

"It went higher in Blackwoods than the few prison guards the DEA initially thought were involved."

"It went all the way to the warden. So how far could the corruption in the DEA go?"

"Far enough to put you in serious danger. I know a place that's safe," he said, "that no one else knows about. I'll take you there."

"And go off alone?" She shook her head.

"I have the gun now," he reminded her.

"*I* don't have a gun," she pointed out. And after what had just happened with the guy running her off the road and abducting her, she didn't trust that the scalpel was enough protection anymore. But even with a gun, she wasn't sure she would feel safe. She wasn't sure she'd feel safe with anyone but Rowe. "You would leave me alone in the city?"

"You went to U of M," he said, which was something else Jed must have told him about her. "You probably spent some time hanging out in Detroit. You know it, and you probably have friends close enough to call. Should I leave you with one of them?"

"You shouldn't leave me at all," she argued, and not just because she was scared but also because she believed he needed her for backup as much as she needed him. "I'm going with you. No matter how far this corruption goes, no one's going to shoot you in the middle of a federal building."

Rowe sighed wearily. "You still haven't accepted that I'm telling you the truth about myself. You don't trust me."

Even though he had saved her life, she couldn't completely trust him because she couldn't completely trust anyone. But that wasn't why she wanted to go along with him. She was scared but not just for herself. She couldn't share all her fears for Jed, and now for him. Somehow, in a very short while, she had begun to care about Rowe. And she didn't want to lose him, too.

DAMN HER. MACY HAD TALKED him into bringing her along to the office. It hadn't been so much what she'd said, though, as it had been the fear and vulnerability in her dark gaze that had compelled him to change his mind. As she'd said, even his betrayer was unlikely to open fire in a federal building. She might be safer here than in his *safe* house.

He turned off the car and reached for the door handle. But she clutched at his arm. "Maybe we shouldn't do this."

"You changed your mind about coming inside?" Relief shuddered through him.

Her fingers tightened on his arm, squeezing. "I changed my mind about your going inside."

He turned to her, confused by her admission. "I

have to. It's the fastest way to figure out who blew my cover—when I see how damn surprised they are that I'm still alive."

"But the minute this person knows you're alive, they'll have their proof that Jed lied to the warden and helped you escape. And then they'll kill him."

If they hadn't already…

But she didn't seem willing to confront that possibility yet. He didn't want to push her and risk hurting her even worse than her attacker had. But he had to be truthful with her.

"I can't stay in hiding the rest of my life," he said. "That would be no kind of life for me. And while it might keep Jed alive, it won't get him out of prison."

And after having spent some time in Blackwoods Penitentiary himself, he suspected that Jed would prefer death to prison. Maybe that—more than his professed innocence—was why the inmate hadn't killed Rowe. Maybe it had been his version of death by cop, only the "cop" was Warden James and was crooked as hell.

"You still don't entirely believe he was framed," she said, the warmth of her brown eyes dimming with disappointment.

He wanted to believe, for her sake. "I have to keep an open mind."

"To his guilt as well as his innocence?"

He nodded. "I can't have my mind already made up or I might miss something when I look over his case files."

She offered him a small smile of appreciation. "But you won't be able to look at his case files unless you go inside your office."

He reached for the door again, and this time she didn't stop him. She just opened her own. "You should stay here," he said.

She shook her head, rejecting his suggestion. "I'm not staying here. Alone."

"You would have the gun," he said, reminding her that he'd put it in the glove box. Since it wasn't registered to him, he wouldn't have gotten the weapon past security. Hell, he would be lucky if *he* made it past security.

Macy met him at the rear of the car and caught his arm, holding tight as if afraid that someone else might try to grab her. Even though he took no pleasure in killing someone, Rowe felt a brief flash of satisfaction that the man who had hurt her would never be able to hurt her again.

"I'd rather have you than the gun," she said.

He met her gaze and something shifted in his chest, his heart clutching in reaction to her words. But she was just scared, for herself and her brother. Once she was safe again, she would forget all about Rowe if she ever forgave him for the pain she had endured because he had caught her up in the danger that was his life.

"Stick close," he said, worried about what would greet them when they walked through the glass doors of the brick federal building. "And keep your head down."

He wore the knit hat, pulled down low over his face. Stubble shadowed his jaw, too, but it was hardly a disguise. As an undercover DEA agent, he looked this way most of the time. So, as he'd feared, he was immediately recognized.

"Hey, Rowe!" one of the guards called out. His old

partner at Detroit P.D. greeted him with a grin as he stepped away from the security monitors. "I heard you quit."

"Quit?" Rowe kept his arm around Macy's shoulders, turning her away from the cameras in the corners of the foyer. He should have left her in the car instead of risking someone getting a hold of security footage and being able to ID her.

"Yeah, I thought your quitting was crazy seeing how you got me this job after Detroit P.D. retired me," the gray-haired former cop replied with a flash of bitterness for his old employer. "The rookie I trained all those years ago would have never left law enforcement. And growing up like you did, the DEA was always your dream job. I didn't think you would ever quit."

Macy glanced up at Rowe, her brow slightly furrowed with a question. With her inquisitive mind, she would want to know exactly how he had grown up. His childhood, or lack thereof, was something Rowe had shared with few people. Donald Jackson had been one of them. Chuck Brennan the other.

The old man chuckled. "I figured the only way you would ever leave this job was in a body bag."

Macy gasped, her eyes sparkling with irony.

Rowe turned back to Chuck. But his old training officer wasn't looking at him; he was looking at Macy. "But then maybe you had a special reason for quitting." The old flirt winked at Macy. "About damn time you got a personal life, Cusack."

Rowe skipped introductions. He didn't want anyone to know who Macy really was; it was bad enough that he had brought her inside where one of the security cameras might have picked up her image.

"Who told you I quit?" he asked, his temper flaring at the lie. His handler would have been the one to concoct and claim the lie as truth. Ostensibly that would have been the only person he could have contacted when he was undercover at Blackwoods. "Agent Jackson?"

"No, he quit, too," Brennan replied, "or at least I think he did since I haven't seen him around here in a while."

"Jackson quit?" His handler had gotten older, but like Brennan, he had never seemed ready to retire. And if he'd quit…

Was it because he had come into a sudden windfall of money? Maybe from the warden…

"Are you going up to the office?" Brennan asked, gesturing toward a break in the line for the security screeners.

Rowe shook his head. "No. I have somewhere else I need to go first."

"But you'll be back, right?" the security guard asked hopefully. "You didn't really quit?"

"Yeah, I'll be back," Rowe promised, and then leaned closer to his old training officer. Pitching his voice low, he added, "But please, do me a favor and don't tell anyone that you saw me today."

"You want them to work to get you back on the job, huh? You're playing hard to get." Brennan chuckled.

"That's the idea." Hard to get and harder to kill.

Brennan slapped Rowe's back. "I knew you wouldn't

be able to stay away, and that all those people around here acting like you'd be gone forever were crazy."

Rowe clenched his jaw and nodded before turning Macy back toward the outside door.

"They acted like you'd be gone forever because they thought you were dead," she murmured as they walked out to the parking lot.

"Yeah, the reports of my demise were greatly exaggerated," he replied, using humor to calm his rising temper.

"If you're going where I think you're headed, those reports may not be exaggerated at all," she warned him. "If this Agent Jackson told the warden to kill you, he won't hesitate to finish the job himself."

That was why Rowe had to drop Macy at the safe house and confront Jackson alone. So that she wouldn't be caught in the cross fire.

ROWE HAD BEEN GONE so long that Macy's heart beat furiously with fear. Something must have happened to him. She was glad that she hadn't let him drop her off wherever he'd been determined to leave her for her *safety*. If he hadn't come back to her at his safe house, she would have had no idea where to look for him. She didn't even know this Agent Jackson's first name or gender let alone where the person lived.

If he or she lived…

And what about Rowe?

But Macy had heard no shots. And she sat in her car, which was parked in the alley behind Jackson's apartment building. She had watched as Rowe had broken into the place. He'd climbed the fire escape and jimmied open a window, keeping watch over her in the alley even more than he had whoever might have been waiting for him in the apartment.

Was that why she'd been able to talk him into letting her come along? Because, after what had happened last time, he didn't want to let her out of his sight. She hadn't wanted him out of her sight either, but she hadn't been able to see him since he had slipped through the open window.

It had been too long.

With trembling fingers, she fumbled the handle and opened the passenger door. Rowe had pulled down the fire escape ladder, but she still had to jump up to reach the bottom rung. Her purse thumped against her side and slipped from her shoulder. She couldn't lose it, not when the only weapon she had was stashed inside the leather bag.

While the alley was empty now, it was strewn with trash that overflowed the Dumpsters. If she hadn't been used to the smells of the morgue, she might have gagged over the stench that hung in the cold spring air. The building was not in the safest area of the city, for sure. But she was less worried about what she might encounter outside than what she would meet up with inside. Her legs shook, with nerves and adrenaline, as she climbed the ladder and then the metal stairs to the fourth-floor apartment.

She had insisted that Rowe bring the gun with him. But if he hadn't had a chance to use it…

Then his betrayer had Rowe's gun and probably at least one of his own.

One with a silencer? Was that why she'd heard no gunshots?

Rowe wouldn't have gone down without a fight. One glance through the window confirmed that there had been a hell of a one. Broken furniture littered the floor. The dining room table and chairs had been smashed. The living room couch was tipped over onto the scarred hardwood. But it was the rug in front of the couch that drew Macy's attention and a gasp from her lips.

A thick, wide pool of blood stained the rug and overflowed onto the hardwood floor. Even if she hadn't had a premed degree, she would know that nobody could have lost that much blood and lived.

Someone had died in this apartment.

Chapter Nine

"I told you to stay in the car," Rowe said, anger bubbling inside him that she hadn't stayed put.

But he was actually angry with himself for not watching over her more closely, so that he had noticed what she was doing before she'd made it up the fire escape to the apartment. While he had been distracted, someone could have pulled her out of the vehicle and driven off with her, just as the guy who had forced her off the road had abducted her. If he hadn't been certain he could keep her safe, he never should have brought her along.

"What happened here?" she asked, as she stepped over the windowsill and joined him inside Donald Jackson's ransacked apartment.

It was bad enough that his prints were going to be all over the place. Now so were hers. "Don't touch anything," he advised.

But she was already kneeling on the floor, dipping her finger into the blood pool. "I thought this was yours," she murmured, her voice shaking with fear. She skimmed her gaze over him, as if checking for injuries. "Whose is it?"

She probably thought that he had killed again and

that he'd been stashing the victim's body somewhere. He had actually been looking for it.

Rowe shrugged. "I don't know for sure if it's Jackson's or someone else's." After his cover had been blown, Rowe had no idea what Donald Jackson was capable of.

"There's no body?" she asked.

He shook his head, but she was already looking away as if afraid to meet his gaze. Rowe studied her face as she examined the blood. Yeah, she probably did think that he had spilled it. He had been inside the apartment long enough to have killed someone. And if Jackson had given him up, he certainly had motive for killing the man.

Revenge.

"This blood is mostly dry, except where it's really deep." Her throat moved as she swallowed hard, as if choking down revulsion. But given that she worked in a morgue, she had to be used to this. Maybe it was fear that was choking her. Fear of him. "It's been here a few days, maybe longer."

"A few days ago I was in prison," he reminded her, hoping to assure her that she was safe with him. He would never hurt her himself. But he wasn't doing a very good job of keeping her safe from harm.

She glanced up at him again and whatever doubts she might have entertained were gone, her brown eyes warm with sympathy. She wasn't just smart, she was intuitive, too, and had picked up on how much it had been bothering Rowe to think that Donald Jackson might have betrayed him.

"Maybe he didn't give you up willingly," she said. "Maybe he was tortured, like Doc...."

By now her brother had probably been tortured, too, since Doc must have talked for the warden to be so convinced that Rowe was still alive.

He shook his head. "I think my cover was blown a while ago. Or maybe it was never really in place. The warden might have known who I was the first day I stepped inside Blackwoods Penitentiary."

If Warden James had a friend or business associate in the DEA, he might have been notified of the administration's investigation into Blackwoods before Rowe had even been assigned to the case. It was a wonder he had survived as long as he had behind bars.

"If the warden knew who you were all that time, you're lucky to be alive," Macy murmured, glancing down at the blood on the floor.

Rowe nodded, wondering how long his luck would hold. He'd spilled some of his blood inside the prison from the wound Jed had inflicted on him. But he hadn't lost nearly this much, only enough to make it look like he could have died.

Was someone playing the same game here? Was someone just pretending to be dead in order to cover up his disappearance—probably heading for a country with no extradition?

"Special Agent Jackson could have given me up," he said, hoping like hell the man he'd considered a friend and a mentor hadn't been bought. "Hell, he could still be alive, too."

Her eyes dark with regret, Macy shook her head.

"There are *pints* of blood here. Nobody could lose this amount of blood and live."

She didn't have her medical degree, but Rowe respected her opinion. If she thought someone had died here, *someone* had died.

"But we don't know that it's Jackson's blood," he pointed out. "Since there's no body, we don't know *who* the hell died here."

"But we know someone died," she insisted.

"This is a crime scene," he said, cupping her elbow to help her to her feet. "And we need to get the hell out. Now."

"*You* were in here awhile," she said. "Looking for the body?"

He nodded. Still holding on to her arm, he led her back to the window. "I was looking for bank statements, too."

"You obviously didn't find the body," she remarked. "What about the bank statements?"

"I only found old ones, not the most recent one." Not the one that would have had the warden's deposit on it if James had paid off Rowe's handler to give up the undercover agent the DEA had sent inside Blackwoods Penitentiary.

"It could be in the mailbox," she suggested. "We could find his key for it and check the box in the building lobby."

Hearing a creaking noise from the hall outside the door, Rowe shook his head. "We can't risk it. We have to go back down the fire escape."

He didn't need to be witnessed leaving a crime scene, especially with Macy. It didn't matter that the blood was old—he and Macy could still be held for questioning. They could even be turned over to the person in the Drug Enforcement Administration who wanted him dead.

After one last glance back at the blood pool, Macy turned toward the window and stepped over the sill onto the metal landing.

Rowe followed her out, peering down into the alley to make sure no one waited below for them. That was when he noticed the Dumpster overflowing with trash. Probably nearly a week or more of garbage topped the Dumpster and fell over the sides. As they descended the steps and then the rungs to the street, he heard the flies buzzing around the metal bin.

"I think I know where the body is," he murmured. He'd noticed the stench earlier but considering the amount of garbage in the alley, he hadn't given it more than a passing thought...until now.

Her attention already on the Dumpster, Macy nodded. "I'll check inside it."

"No, I'll check it out," he said, the muscles in his stomach clenching and tightening with foreboding. He wasn't going to like what he found inside that metal bin. "You get in the car."

"But I have the medical education—"

"You already said nobody could have lost that much blood and survived," he reminded her. It wasn't like she was going to be able to save whoever he found, and he was pretty damn sure that he was going to find someone. At least whatever was left of him or her...

"I also have experience in the coroner's office, remember?" she argued. "I can check out the body and determine cause of death."

"I don't know what's in that Dumpster." And he wasn't really crazy about digging through all that trash himself, but he certainly wasn't going to let her do it. "There are probably dirty needles in there." He'd learned young how to avoid those. "And God knows what else."

And all his instincts were warning him that something bad was about to happen. So he waited until she opened the car door before he stepped closer to the Dumpster.

Holding his breath, he leaned over the rusted metal side and began to dig through the mess. He had to toss out boxes and garbage bags before he found the body.

Jackson's skin was pale with just a bluish tinge except for the gaping wound in his chest that had turned from red to black from dried blood and flies.

He gagged and turned away to find Macy next to him. "It's him," he told her. "It's Donald Jackson. My handler."

His mentor, too. Guilt twisted his guts more than the god-awful smell. Why had he been so quick to suspect Jackson of betraying him? Sure, around the same age he'd learned to avoid used needles he had learned to trust no one, but Jackson had cared about the job. Like Rowe, he had been dedicated to getting drugs off the streets.

Donald Jackson hadn't betrayed Rowe. He had been betrayed…and murdered.

"He's been dead for a few days," Macy said, from what she could observe of the body by rising on her tiptoes and peering inside the Dumpster. "Looks like he was shot in the chest." With a cannon. At least more than one shot had been fired into this man. Decomposition had caused the rest of the damage to the wound.

"Looks like," Rowe agreed, his already deep voice husky with emotion.

He had obviously cared about this man. He had been more than just a coworker to Rowe. He had been his lifeline to the outside when he'd gone undercover. She couldn't imagine how he must have felt believing this man had given him up to the warden.

Rowe moved more garbage off him, as if in respect. "He was also beaten."

Like Doc. Tortured.

"He's holding something," Macy remarked, as she noticed the wallet clutched in the man's hand. Had he taken a bribe? Had it been the last thing he had ever done?

Rowe reached in and tugged the leather bifold free of the dead man's grasp. Then he flipped it open to a photo and a badge smeared with blood. The face in the picture didn't belong to the man in the alley. The agent in the photo was young and blond and handsome: Special Agent Rowe Cusack. "It's my credentials."

"He had them?"

"He's my handler. He held on to them when I went undercover." A muscle twitched beneath the dark blond stubble on Rowe's tightly clenched jaw. "He had my gun, too. Hell, he was probably shot with it."

"You were in prison," she reminded him. "You're not responsible for this. And whatever gun the killer used must have had a silencer on it since no one called the police."

He glanced around the empty alley and sighed wearily. "Nobody calls the police around here."

She peered up at him, puzzled by how certain he sounded. Had this been his beat when he was Detroit P.D. with the security guard back at the federal building? Or, like his handler, did he live around here?

Or had he grown up around here? Was that what the security guard meant when he'd mentioned that how Rowe had grown up had made him so determined to be an agent with the DEA?

"You know this area?" she asked.

He nodded. "Grew up here." He pointed toward some of the apartment buildings backed up to the alley. "And there. And there. And there..."

"You moved around a lot?" she asked, wondering about the childhood that had made Rowe's job so important to him.

"Got tossed out of a lot of apartments and crashed in a lot of them after getting tossed out."

"How old were you?"

He shrugged. "I don't know. It was a long time ago."

She hated the thought of Rowe living in such a neighborhood now, but especially as a kid, nearly as much as she hated the thought of Jed locked up. In a way growing up here would have been like serving life in prison because so many kids never made it out of rough neighborhoods like this. Like the inmates in Blackwoods Penitentiary, so many died inside.

"But I still know how life is around here," he continued. "No one calls the police."

"Nobody calls even when guns are being fired?" she asked, realizing now how sheltered her life had been, how sheltered it still was even after her brother's unjust arrest.

Rowe chuckled, albeit with no amusement. "Guns are always being fired around here."

And as if to prove his point, gunshots echoed within the alley and pinged off the metal next to her head. A cry of surprise and fear slipped through her lips.

MACY'S CRY STRUCK ROWE'S HEART like the bullets nearly struck her head. He grabbed her, pulling her tight against him as he leaned over her to shield her. The gunshots came from above, probably from the fire escape outside Jackson's apartment. The creaking he'd heard in the hall hadn't been someone on their way to their own apartment but the killer returning to the scene of his crime.

Since the shooter had the vantage point of being several floors above them, Rowe and Macy were sitting ducks in the alley. He hunched down over Macy as he pushed her toward the car. Bullets glanced off the Dumpster and ground into the asphalt near their feet as they ran. Rowe pulled open the driver's door and shoved her inside, across the driver's seat and over the console.

Glass shattered, the windshield exploding as bullets struck it. The rear window went next, shards of glass spreading like confetti across the asphalt. More bullets dented the roof.

He pushed her onto the floorboards beneath the dash. "Stay down!"

His hand shaking, he jammed the key in the ignition. If it had been just him, he would have returned fire. He would have brought down the son of a bitch firing at them. But now, with Macy in danger, all he could think about was getting her to safety. And it had nothing to do with his promise to Jed and everything to do with his own feelings for her.

After a sputter, the car started. He jerked the shifter into Reverse and started backing out of the alley. But the gunman was coming down the escape, the shots getting closer. Rowe slowed for a quick glance, but before he could get a good look at the shooter, the side window exploded.

Shards of glass rained down on Macy. She screamed again in surprise and fear.

"Stay down!" he shouted. Pressing hard on the accelerator, he steered the car backward out of the narrow alley and straight into traffic on the busy urban street.

Horns blared and bumpers crunched against metal as a couple of cars collided with her little coupe. Rowe didn't stop. He shifted into Drive and merged into the busy traffic. The dented metal rubbed against the tire, burning the rubber, and he could barely see through the shattered shards left of the windshield.

"Are you okay?" he asked, anger and adrenaline coursing through him.

She didn't reply.

"Macy?" He tore his gaze from the traffic and glanced down at her. Blood streaked over her face. She had been hit. "Macy!"

THE WARDEN NEARLY IGNORED the ringing phone. But it was that damn untraceable cell and only one person had that number—his suddenly not-so-silent silent partner.

He grabbed the phone and shouted, "I don't have time for this."

"You're going to have to make time, or you're going to lose everything."

James glanced at the pictures on the wall, specifically at the one of his daughter's smiling face. Her blue eyes brimmed with happiness and love as if she'd known he would look at it as often as he did. Would she look at him like that if she knew everything about her daddy? The frame was still hanging crooked; he had yet to straighten it.

He was afraid he was already losing everything; he could feel it all slipping away. "I told you that I can't find Cusack's body."

"That's because he's not dead."

He cursed even though he wasn't surprised. After Doc had declared the undercover inmate dead, the head guard had stopped the old physician at the gates with all his personal stuff and records packed to leave. He'd known too much to just let him go—all about James's operation. He had also known what had really happened to the DEA agent. But he had taken that information to his grave.

"You're sure?" James asked. The guy had definitely been hurt, maybe bad enough that he hadn't survived his injuries.

"I saw him myself," his partner verified. "He's here in Detroit."

He breathed a sigh of relief that the DEA agent was

no longer his problem. "That's good. Then you can take care of him."

"I tried," was the sharp reply. "I emptied a couple of clips, but I don't think I even hit the son of a bitch once."

"You said he was good," Warden recalled. "But I thought you were better."

"I *am* better," the agent insisted. "But Rowe Cusack is a survivor. I warned you that he wouldn't be easy to kill."

"It may not be easy, but it's not impossible." No one was as strong and indestructible as they thought they were; not even James.

"At least I think I hit the girl."

"Damn, I need that girl alive." Macy Kleyn might have been the only way to end the situation at the prison before it escalated even further, beyond the warden's control.

"I've been monitoring all the hospitals and clinics for gunshot wounds," the special agent said, "and he hasn't brought her in for medical treatment."

"So she's dead." *Damn it!*

"If she is, that's a good thing. She's been helping Cusack," the agent reminded him, "so she knows too much."

"True," the warden agreed. "But I still need her here."

"She may only be injured. He got away fast," James's partner said with respect for the other agent, "too fast for me to follow him."

"You have to figure out where he is," James said. He

already had a situation inside the prison; he didn't need to worry about trouble brewing outside of it, too.

"You need to get Cusack back up there before he talks," the special agent ordered.

And James was getting damn sick of taking orders and taking the blame for what hadn't been entirely his idea.

"Right now he doesn't know who to trust."

James could relate to the DEA agent's predicament. He didn't know who to trust either. "Cusack trusted the girl."

"If she's gone, he's going to have to turn to someone else."

"You?"

"Let's hope," the agent said.

Hope was all Jefferson could do. He used to pray too, but when those prayers had gone unanswered, he'd given up on asking anyone else for help. And he'd started taking care of everything himself.

"But he might turn to the other inmate who helped him get out of Blackwoods," the DEA agent suggested.

Despite his offices being on the other end of the building from the cell blocks and common areas, noise echoed out in the hall. Shouts. Gunshots. "That won't be possible."

"James, what's going on?"

"Nothing I can't handle," he assured his partner.

"You couldn't handle Rowe Cusack," he was taunted for his failure.

"Neither could you."

"That's why we need to work together to eliminate him as a threat once and for all."

Warden James sighed but agreed, "Rowe Cusack is a dead man."

"Not yet, but like his girlfriend, he will soon be dead."

Chapter Ten

"I'm fine," Macy assured Rowe. And she actually was fine now that he'd gotten them away from the alley and the gunfire and to that safe location he had been wanting to bring her to since they had arrived in the city.

Concern dimmed the brightness of his light blue eyes as he studied her face. "You need to go to the emergency room."

"We can't risk it," she reminded him. "And it's totally unnecessary. It's only a shallow scratch. Some broken glass grazed me."

"But you lost consciousness," he reminded her, brushing hair from her face. "You could have a concussion."

She smiled at his overblown reaction. "I did not lose consciousness. I just closed my eyes for a minute to catch my breath. I heard you." His voice had sounded as if he were a long distance away, though, instead of just a couple of feet. But she'd pulled it together, maybe even a little faster than he had.

His fingers shook slightly as he cupped her face and studied the scratches on her forehead. "You're really all right?"

"As long as no one shoots at me again for a while,

I'll be fine." She was shaking, too, in reaction to all she had gone through…and survived.

"You'll be safe here," he assured her. "This is where I wanted to bring you the minute we got close to Detroit."

They weren't that near Detroit, though. After he'd pulled off the street to make sure she was okay, he'd driven awhile before they had reached this abandoned airfield and the airplane hangar in which he'd parked her car.

He had lost her with the circuitous route he'd taken, so he had undoubtedly lost whoever might have tried to follow them.

"What is this place?" she asked. Half of the hangar had been converted to a loftlike apartment with high metal ceilings and cement floors. A kitchenette took up part of one wall while a bed stood in the middle of the cavernous room.

"It was a mobster's private airfield and personal airplane hangar."

"That makes me feel safe," she quipped.

"It is a safe house," he assured her. "Now."

She shivered, chilled despite the wall unit furnace that blew heat into the open space. "That depends on how many people know about it."

"Just me."

"You've never used it to keep anyone safe?" she asked.

That muscle twitched along his jaw now. "Once," he admitted. "I brought a witness here."

"So the witness would know about it," she pointed

out, and then someone in the DEA might have learned about it, too. Suddenly she felt a whole lot less safe.

"The witness didn't make it."

She glanced around, looking for bullet holes in the walls. But the light was fading outside and Rowe had yet to turn on the fluorescent lights that hung from the rafters. "How safe is it then?"

"I got the witness to court," he said. But he spoke with no pride, only regret.

"And someone killed her there?"

"Him. Yeah. A bailiff killed him."

She had a feeling that the bailiff hadn't made it out of court either that day. Rowe would have done whatever necessary to try to save his witness, like he had put himself directly into the line of fire to protect her. The thought of him taking a bullet for her chilled her to the bone, and she shivered.

He moved away from her and turned up the blower on the wall unit furnace. "It'll warm up in here soon," he assured her. "I stay here every once in a while when I want to get away from the congestion of the city."

She glanced at the things spread around the room and suspected he stayed here more than once in a while. "How far from the city are we?"

He expelled a weary sigh. "Not far enough."

"How did someone know we were there?" she wondered then gasped as she realized how. "Your friend— that security guard—he must have told someone that we stopped by the DEA building."

Rowe gave a grim nod. "I need to find out who he talked to after we left. You'll be safe here." He headed toward the steel door that opened onto the other half of the hangar where he'd parked her battered car next to a newer pickup truck. "I'll be back."

She grabbed his arm and held tightly on to the hard muscles beneath her fingers. "No."

"You don't think I'll come back?"

Her heart pounded fast and furiously with fear as she remembered those incessant shots. "Someone's trying to kill you."

"They haven't succeeded yet," he said with a flash of pride and sheer stubbornness glinting in his blue eyes.

She understood stubbornness since she was so often accused of being it herself. But there was stubbornness and then there was stubbornness. "They will succeed if you keep giving them opportunities."

"I already told you that I can't stay in hiding the rest of my life," he reminded her.

"Not the rest of your life," she agreed. "Just the rest of tonight. Stay here—" she stepped closer to the long, hard length of his body "—with me."

Tears stung her eyes as emotion and exhaustion overwhelmed her. It had been a hell of a day; she didn't want to spend the night alone. She wanted to spend it with Rowe. In his arms.

ROWE'S GUTS TWISTED. He wanted to stay. Hell, he just wanted her. But he couldn't take advantage of her fear and vulnerability. "You'll be safe here," he promised.

"You're so concerned with keeping me safe," she murmured, "at the risk of your own life. Is that just because it's your job?"

He had taken his shield from the crime scene; it was in his pocket now, smeared with Jackson's blood. But that wasn't the reason for his concern for her safety. It was because he cared about her, more than he had a right to care. He couldn't burden her with his feelings, not when he was a man with a price on his head. So he told her, "I made your brother a promise."

"You promised Jed to keep me safe?" She stepped back from him, and the color fled from her face, leaving her skin pale but for the cut and the bruise on her jaw and the dried blood on her forehead.

"I made him the promise," he clarified, "but I haven't been carrying it out very damn well."

"Jed shouldn't have been worried about me. He should have been worried about himself." Her breath caught, and her eyes welled with tears she was too strong to shed. "Do you think he's okay?"

Rowe had his doubts, but he couldn't share those with her; she was too vulnerable right now. "Your brother is smart. Nearly as smart as you are."

She smiled. "Jed's smarter than I am. He figured out that I was dyslexic before anyone else did. I just thought I was stupid." Her smile faded. "So did our parents."

His heart clutched at the pain she must have endured as a misunderstood kid. "Jed is smart," he agreed. "So he had to know that eventually it would come out that he helped me instead of killed me."

"So what are you saying?" she asked, her bruised chin lifting in stubborn pride. "Are you saying that he didn't care about his own life? That helping you was his way of committing suicide?"

The thought had crossed Rowe's mind. But if Jedidiah Kleyn had half the guts his sister did, he wasn't a quitter. "Your brother doesn't strike me as the type who'd give up that easily. He's a fighter."

His ribs still ached where Jed Kleyn's big fists had struck him, and the stitches itched where his knife wound had already began to heal, the burning pain reduced to only a dull throb now.

"Jed is a fighter," she agreed. "Hell, he's a decorated war hero. But he's one man against the entire prison. He's alone in there."

Rowe shook his head. "No, *I* was alone in there. Jedidiah Kleyn is a legend. The other inmates respect him. They'll have his back."

"What happened to there being no honor among thieves?" She snorted in derision of his claim. "Convicted killers and drug dealers will go against the warden to help my brother? You're lying to me."

She didn't understand what it was like in Blackwoods. Hell, neither had he really. But Jed had been there for three years, lasting longer than a lot of other inmates had inside the notorious penitentiary. "Macy—"

She pressed her fingers over his lips, stemming his argument. "Save your breath. I know you're just trying to ease my fears."

"I do want to ease your fears," he admitted. He wanted to wrap her up in his arms and protect her from pain. "But I'm not lying to you."

"Thank you." She replaced her fingers with her lips, rising up on tiptoe to kiss him. "Thank you...."

His breath catching in his lungs as his heart slammed against his ribs, he fought for control and pulled back. He didn't deserve her gratitude. He didn't deserve her.

"What the hell are you thanking me for? I've nearly gotten you killed more than once." And he had probably already gotten her brother killed.

"Thank you for *saving* me."

Somehow he suspected she wasn't just talking about his saving her from the man in the shed or from the bullets in the alley. "Macy…?"

"Even though I moved up to Blackwoods to be close to Jed, I've felt so lonely there. I've had no one to talk to. My parents thought I was crazy to believe and support Jed. So did my ex."

He flinched, wanting to ask her about this ex, but he didn't want to interrupt her when she'd obviously needed to talk for a while. Three years…

"After the way they had all acted, I didn't dare tell anyone about Jed. I was so alone." Her breath caught and then shuddered out in a shaky little sigh as she stepped closer to Rowe. "Until I unzipped that body bag with you inside."

"You saved me then," he admitted. "I thought I was going to die in there."

"If it had been zipped up all the way, you might have, but Doc had left breathing room," she said.

A gasp slipped through his lips, as it nearly had when he'd been lying inside that damn bag. "Not enough…"

Her eyes narrowed as she studied his face. "You didn't like the drawer either. I thought it was just because it was creepy—"

"It was creepy." He shuddered in remembrance of the cold metal drawer.

She glanced at the high ceilings of the hangar and his

belongings scattered around the place. She must have realized he spent more than a little time at the hangar. "You really don't like enclosed places."

"No. I spent too much time in them when I was a kid," he admitted.

"Your fr— That security guard mentioned that how you grew up is what compels you to care so much about your job."

She had stopped herself from calling Brennan his friend. What was Brennan? His betrayer? Or just a man who always said too much like he had in front of Macy.

But after everything they'd been through together, he didn't mind her knowing what he'd rarely shared with anyone else. "My parents were drug addicts," he admitted. "When I was a little kid, they'd lock me up in a closet while they and their friends were using."

He had spent hours, sometimes days, locked up.

She gasped now. "I'm so sorry." Her arms slid around his waist and she pressed herself against his chest. "It must have been so horrible for you getting zipped into that bag, and then me shutting you in the drawer. I'm so sorry."

He couldn't resist her anymore. He might have been taking advantage of her current state of vulnerability, but he wasn't strong enough to fight his own desires.

And he had never desired anyone the way he did Macy Kleyn. She was so smart and so damn sexy. He lowered his head and really kissed her. Not just that teasing brush of lips. Instead his mouth pressed hungrily against hers. Her lips were silky, her breath warm as a moan slipped out of her. He parted her lips and deepened the kiss, sliding his tongue into the sweet moistness of her mouth.

Her tongue flicked across his, tasting him. She moaned again, and her fingers clutched his nape, tunneling through his hair.

He touched her hair too, tugging the binding free so that the soft sable strands tangled around his fingers. Then he cupped the back of her head in his hand, and he could feel the faint ridge of her old scar against his palm. Even as a kid, she had been undefeatable.

As a woman she was fierce. She pulled away from him slightly before she clutched his shirt, pulling it up and over his head. Then she skimmed her fingers down his arms until she caught his hands in hers and tugged him toward the bed.

He trapped her between the mattress and his body, holding her still for his kiss. He made love to her mouth. Then he moved to her body. Lifting her sweater, he pulled it over her head. His breath escaped in another gasp of horror when he saw the bruise on her ribs.

"He hit you." That son of a bitch who'd run her off the road and abducted her had struck more than her beautiful face.

She shook her head, tousling her hair around her bare shoulders, and corrected him. "He kicked me."

"He's lucky he's already dead." Or Rowe would kill him again.

She shivered. And he regretted scaring her. But her fear didn't last, because she reached for his belt next, tugging it free to unsnap his jeans. He sucked in a breath when her fingers glided over his abs then dipped inside the waistband of his boxers.

"Macy…"

She bit her bottom lip. "I really want *this*. I really want *you*."

Was she trying to convince him or herself?

"Are you sure?" he asked, because with every touch of her soft hands, he was getting closer and closer to totally losing control.

She bit her bottom lip and nodded. "It's about the only thing I am sure of right now."

He understood that. With all the doubts, suspicions and betrayals in his world right now, she was the only one he could count on. The only one he could hang on to. But before he could close his arms around her, she reached behind herself.

So used to people betraying him, he braced himself for a minute, not knowing what she was reaching for. It could have been that vicious little scalpel again. But then her bra dropped onto the floor, and he realized she'd just undone the clasp. Her jeans followed, as she unsnapped and shimmied out of those and her cotton panties. She stood before him completely naked and completely vulnerable, her wide eyes dark with desire and nerves.

"It's been a while for me," she admitted, her voice shaky with those nerves. "But I—I think you need to get rid of your jeans, too." She reached for his zipper.

But he stepped back. He just wanted to stare at her, to drink in every inch of her silky flesh and soft curves. It was himself he didn't trust right now. Because if he let her touch him, he might lose all control and take her with all the passion burning inside him for her.

And she had already been handled too roughly. She deserved a gentleness he wasn't even sure he was capable of.

MACY SHIVERED AGAIN, TREMBLING at the intense look in his light blue eyes.

"What's the matter?" she asked. Had he changed his mind? Had she totally repulsed him?

His breath shuddered out in a ragged sigh. "You are so damn beautiful…"

Bruised and battered, she felt anything but beautiful until she met his gaze. Desire heated the normal icy blue of his eyes, making them glow in the fading light.

Then he kissed her again, deeply. And his hands moved over her, gently, just skimming across her skin. He touched every inch of her and his mouth followed the path of his hands, kissing the curve of her shoulder, the inside of her elbow, the back of her knee…until she trembled so much with desire that her legs wouldn't hold her weight. She fell back onto the mattress.

She lay there alone but just until he finally unzipped and dropped his jeans. She gasped at the masculine beauty of him. Since she had spent so much of her life studying, she hadn't done much dating and had had only one lover, the man she had thought she would marry one day. She'd had her whole life planned out.

She hadn't planned on Rowe Cusack and the feelings that he elicited from her. Just looking at his masculine perfection—all the rippling muscles under sleek skin—had her nipples peaking and an intense pressure winding tight inside her.

Then he joined her, covering her body with his. He

kissed her lips and then skimmed his mouth down her throat to the curve of her breast. His lips closed over one tight nipple, tugging gently before he stroked the peak with his tongue.

She shifted beneath him as the pressure wound even tighter, unbearably tighter. Instinctively seeking to release it, she arched her hips against his. But he was in no hurry. He took his time with both breasts, thoroughly teasing each nipple.

She clutched at his head, first holding him against her and then trying to pull him away. But instead of moving his mouth up, back to hers, he shifted lower, skimming his lips down her stomach. He gently kissed the bruised skin and then moved lower, between her legs. He loved her with his mouth, his tongue stroking her until an orgasm shuddered through her.

The aftershocks rippled inside her, but then he was there, his erection pushing against the very core of her. She arched and stretched, trying to take him deeper. But he was so hard, so thick. She shifted and clutched at his back, and then his butt, writhing beneath him as the pressure built again.

He thrust in and out, driving her closer and closer to the edge of complete insanity. And finally the madness claimed her. She screamed his name as she came.

He thrust a few more times, harder and deeper, until he tensed and joined her in the madness. A groan tore from his throat as he buried himself deep inside her and clutched her close. He rolled, though, so that she was on top, lying across his slick chest, which rose and fell with his labored breaths.

His voice gruff with passion, he tried to talk. "That was…"

Beyond anything she had ever experienced before. It didn't matter to Macy that her experience was limited; she knew that what they had just shared was special. So special that guilt tugged at her. "I'm sorry…."

His hands, which had been stroking her back, stilled. "You're sorry?"

"Not about this," she assured him. She had never been less sorry about anything in her life. Making love with Rowe was the last thing she would regret. "I'm sorry that I haven't told you everything."

He arched a golden-blond brow. "Are you married?" he teased with the knowledge that she wasn't.

Jed had certainly told him a lot about her. Jed…

She couldn't think about her brother right now. She would have to face those fears later.

"I should be," she admitted. It had been part of her plan. "But my ex-fiancé…" Or almost fiancé since he hadn't actually bought the ring yet. "My ex-fiancé dumped me when I wouldn't turn my back on Jed."

And worry that Rowe would turn his back on her brother was what had kept her from admitting everything to him.

"He was a fool," he declared of a man he had never met.

Not that Macy thought he was wrong.

"He thought I was the fool," she said. "Dr. Bernard and the warden think I'm a fool, too." Even her own parents had thought she was.

"Well, you can't believe anything the warden tells

you," he said. "The man's a liar and a cold-blooded killer."

She sucked in a breath, bracing herself for her question. "Then you don't believe that my brother killed Doc?"

Beneath her, his body tensed. "What?"

"That's what Warden James told Dr. Bernard. That Jed killed Doc." She gazed up at his face, silently begging him to call the warden a liar again.

But he hesitated.

"You don't believe that Jed did?" she asked anxiously. Because if Rowe believed, then she might begin to doubt her brother, too. He hadn't committed the crimes of which he'd been charged. But since his conviction, he had been locked up with killers.

Had he become one?

Rowe spoke slowly as if choosing his words carefully. "If Jed thought that Doc might talk and betray him…"

"Jed wouldn't hurt someone even to protect himself." She knew her brother better than that; prison couldn't have changed him that much from the honorable, protective man he had always been.

A twinge of guilt clutched her heart that she had doubted him even for a moment. She shouldn't have said anything to Rowe, because she couldn't have him doubting Jed either…because then he might decide against helping him.

"You wouldn't be here if Jed was concerned with protecting himself," she reminded him, "because he would have chosen to kill you instead of going against the warden."

"Do I think Jed would kill someone to protect himself?" Rowe asked, and shook his head in reply to his own question. "Probably not. But your brother would do anything to protect *you*."

That was what she was afraid of—that Jed might have killed for her. She blinked back tears of regret, that her presence in Blackwoods had forced him to protect her, and disillusionment that her brother could hurt anyone. Even for her.

Offering comfort and protection, Rowe's strong arms closed tightly around her. "I would do anything to protect you, too…"

She didn't know what scared her more—that men would kill for her. Or that, in trying to kill to protect her, they might die instead.

Chapter Eleven

Protecting Macy meant locking her inside a safe house so that she wouldn't insist on putting herself in the line of fire as she had in the alley.

Rowe had waited until she'd fallen asleep before leaving her. Of course he'd had to wait and make certain that she was deeply asleep before he'd crawled out of the warm bed they had shared. He might have also been savoring the feeling of her in his arms, curled against his chest, her heart thudding in perfect rhythm with his.

Leaving her had been one of the hardest things he'd ever done. But if he really wanted to protect her, he had to eliminate the threat to her safety. And *he* was nearly as much a threat as the warden and whoever had betrayed him to the warden.

Inside another house, back in the city, Rowe stepped out of the shadows. Then, with his target in sight, he cocked his gun.

Brennan jerked awake, in the recliner where he'd fallen asleep in front of the TV. A beer clutched in his hand, he fumbled with the can, spilling it over his T-shirt before reaching for the weapon he'd left on the end table. But Rowe already had that in his hand.

"What the hell—" his old partner and training officer grumbled, brushing his hand over his face as if he couldn't believe he was really seeing Rowe in his living room.

Had he thought he would be dead by now? That some of those bullets in the alley had struck him?

"You seem surprised to see me," Rowe remarked bitterly.

Brennan shuddered. "What the hell is the matter with you that you'd break into my place like this, pointing a gun at me!"

"You know," Rowe challenged him to admit to his duplicity.

The retired cop shook his head. "I have no idea what's going on with you. First you quit the job you've always wanted—"

"I didn't quit," Rowe vehemently denied. "And you already know that."

The older man sighed. "Damn. Damn it. I knew it wasn't right, that something was going on…"

"You knew that I would never quit the DEA." Not when it was all he'd talked about when he'd been a naive rookie with Detroit P.D.

"At first, I figured that your *quitting* must have been part of a cover for a new assignment," Brennan said. "And I don't have the clearance to know what's going on inside the DEA. I don't even *want* to know."

"But you know that something's going on," Rowe reminded him of what he'd just admitted. "What the hell is it?"

Brennan shrugged. "I don't know. A lot of people just seem really anxious about you. Someone must have spotted you in the lobby today…" He glanced to the light streaking through his living room blinds. "Yesterday…"

"You know about the shots fired at me." And Macy. He flinched as he remembered the blood trickling down her pale face. For a moment he thought she'd been killed. "In the alley behind Jackson's apartment."

Brennan gasped. "Hell, no, I didn't know about that! Was that little gal with you then?"

Rowe nodded.

"Is she all right?"

"She's safe." In spite of him, not *because* of him. "If you didn't know about the shots, how do *you* know that someone spotted me?"

"After what you said, about keeping quiet about seeing you," Brennan reminded him, "I intended to erase the security footage from when you were there."

"That could have gotten you fired," Rowe warned him with a flash of guilt that he'd doubted his former law enforcement teacher.

The older man shrugged. "Doesn't matter now. It got pulled and sent up to your old department before I could erase it."

"Do you know who ordered it?"

He shook his gray-haired head. "Only a few agents had cleared security and were up on your floor when it was ordered."

"Who?"

Brennan sighed. "This could get me fired, too, sharing classified information with an ex-agent." But he didn't hesitate before adding, "Tillman, Hernandez and O'Neil."

Rowe cursed. "They're all good agents."

Damn good agents with more years of experience than he had, and a lot more connections in the hierarchy of the Drug Enforcement Administration. Rowe couldn't accuse any one of them of corruption without some damn compelling evidence.

"What's going on, kid?" Brennan asked, weariness spreading more lines across his face.

"The less you know the better…" Or his old training officer might wind up like Jackson and Doc. And probably Jed Kleyn…

Brennan gestured toward the gun Rowe clutched yet in one hand. "So I wasn't wrong to think I might need that tonight?"

"No, you weren't wrong," Rowe said, confirming that the older man's instincts were as sharp as they had ever been. "If someone saw you talking to me, you could be in danger."

"That's what I thought," Brennan agreed. His hand shaking and sloshing what was left of his beer, he set the can on the table next to his chair. "That's why I was sitting up, trying to stay awake, so I'd be ready if anyone came after me." He wearily shook his head in self-disgust over his failure. "Maybe Detroit P.D. was right to retire me."

Rowe wanted to make sure that his friend's retirement didn't become permanent. "You need to get out of here," he said. "Get yourself someplace safe until I tell you it's all over."

He didn't want to lose anyone else who mattered to him. He didn't want anyone else losing his life because of him….

"You got that girl stashed someplace like that?" Brennan asked. "Someplace none of those agents can find her?"

He had thought he had...until he'd learned which agents might have betrayed him.

Tillman had military experience in addition to all his years with DEA. He had carried out countless special ops, bringing back intel that had saved many lives.

Hernandez had gone deeper undercover than any other agent, spending years with drug cartels that had cut off heads and cut out hearts of people they'd only suspected were informants. He was brilliant and slick.

O'Neil worked twice as hard as every other agent, determined to prove herself smarter and stronger than any male agent. And she had proved herself over and over again with arrests that no one else could have pulled off.

If he'd been considered a potential threat, any one of them could have been tracking his prior movements and found his private safe house.

And Rowe had left Macy locked up inside. She was alone and defenseless. Sure, she was tough and smart and resilient. But that had been against a warden of a backwater prison and a drug addict—not against a trained and experienced DEA agent.

FOR THE SECOND TIME in less than twenty-four hours, pain awakened Macy. It throbbed along her swollen jaw and ached in her stomach where she'd been kicked. Twinges of pain even pulled at her back and her neck and shoulders from the impact her body had absorbed when the SUV had rear-ended her van.

But then she had other aches, delicious aches in places she hadn't been touched in so long and never as deeply as Rowe had touched her. She stretched, spreading her arms wide across the mattress, reaching for him so that he could make her hurt in another way. In a wicked, wonderful way...

But her hands patted only tangled blankets and sheets. He was gone.

She opened her eyes and looked around the cavernous room. Sunlight streaked through a narrow window that was at least twenty feet above the cement floor. The light was bright enough to illuminate the wide-open space and the bed that was empty of anyone but her.

She glanced toward the bathroom that was tucked into a corner of the hangar; the door stood fully open. Nobody was inside shaving at the sink or standing in the glass-walled shower.

"Rowe?" Her voice echoed off the open rafters and metal ceiling. "Rowe!"

He'd left her. He had made love to her and then he'd just left her alone?

Had it been a trick, a way to distract her so that he could get away from her?

"Damn you!" She threw back the covers and grabbed up the clothes she had dropped onto the cold cement floor next to the bed.

She had undressed for him. She had begged him to stay with her, to make love with her. Heat rushed to her face, adding to the pain in her jaw, as embarrassment consumed her. She'd thrown herself at the man.

Did he know why, that it was because she was beginning to have feelings for him? Or did he think it was just another thing, that *he* was just another thing she'd done to get her brother out of prison?

He had been curiously quiet after she'd told him about the warden's accusation that Jed had killed Doc. Had he changed his mind about helping her brother? Had he changed his mind about her?

She glanced out the window to the unfinished half of the metal hangar and noticed her car, with its broken windows, was the only vehicle left in the space. The truck, she'd noticed when he'd brought her to the hangar, was gone.

She hurriedly dressed and headed toward the door. But when she tried the knob, it refused to budge. The lock was the kind that could only be opened with a key. He had locked her inside?

She turned toward the window, but the one to the outside was up too high on the wall for her to reach even if she piled furniture up beneath it. And the window that opened onto the other half of the hangar was reinforced with a steel grid and what was probably bulletproof glass. She wouldn't be able to break it to free herself.

"Son of a bitch…"

What kind of safe house was this?

The kind that kept a witness in as well as the criminals out. No wonder he hadn't lost the witness; the guy hadn't been able to run. And neither could Macy. Why would Rowe do this to her?

Didn't he trust her? Probably not. He didn't seem to trust anyone but then he had good reason not to. And so did she, after her brother had been framed.

She should have known better than to trust Rowe Cusack, let alone fall asleep in his arms. Heat rushed back to her face, warming her despite the chill in the air. She headed toward the wall unit furnace and cranked up the blowers. What if she were to shove some paper in where the pilot light glowed? What would happen if the place caught fire?

She glanced up at the smoke detectors. They weren't just plastic, a battery and wires. There was a digital panel on them, something programmed into them. So if she caught the place on fire, maybe the door would automatically open...

But what if it didn't? Was burning to death a risk she was willing to take? The alternative was waiting and trusting that Rowe would come back for her. She wasn't sure that was a risk she was willing to take either. Before she could make her decision, a phone jangled. It couldn't have been hers. Rowe had had her leave that back in the van just in case someone traced the GPS on it. But the ringing emanated from her purse. She reached inside, shoving aside her wallet with the scalpel tucked inside it, for the phone that lit up beneath it.

Mr. Mortimer's cell phone. Rowe had left it for her instead of taking it with him. She didn't recognize the number on the caller ID, but she suspected she knew who it was. "You damn well better be coming back," she warned her missing lover.

"No, Miss Kleyn," a man said, his voice bone-chillingly cold, "*you* better be coming back."

"Who is this?" she asked.

"I think you know," the warden replied, too smart to identify himself.

How had he realized that she'd taken the phone from Mr. Mortimer's personal effects?

Dr. Bernard must have discovered the cell missing. But instead of reporting her theft to the sheriff, he had reported it to the warden. Was her former employer part of the corruption and cover-up at Blackwoods Penitentiary?

Betrayal clutched her heart. She had felt horrible for the secrets she'd kept from her boss. But now she suspected she hadn't been the only one keeping secrets.

Dr. Bernard must not have reported all the deaths at Blackwoods Penitentiary, or there would have been an investigator before Rowe sent to the prison. Had he kept quiet because he was afraid of the warden or because he was being reimbursed to keep his silence? How much money had he received to give up the information about her? Enough to make it worth her life?

"What do you want with me?" she asked. "I already told you everything I know."

"It's not so much *what* you know as *who* you know," the warden replied.

"I don't understand what you're talking about…"

"Your brother, for one, Miss Kleyn," he replied. "We need to talk about your brother."

"What about Jed?"

"Come to Blackwoods Penitentiary," he ordered her, "and we'll discuss your brother."

"Is he all right?" Or was it already too late for him?

"He won't be *anything* much longer, Miss Kleyn," he warned her. "You need to hurry back. No matter how badly you're hurt, your brother will be hurt worse if you don't show up."

How did he know that she had left Blackwoods County? Whoever had been shooting at her and Rowe in the alley must have called the warden. And like Rowe had for a brief time, they thought one of all those flying bullets had struck her.

Despite how close she stood to the furnace, she shivered. "I'm not hurt. Your lackey wasn't a very good shot."

"That's good," he said, a breath rattling the phone almost as if he'd breathed a sigh of relief that she was unharmed. Probably just because *he* wanted to be the one who hurt her. "Then you have no excuse not to hurry back here."

"Before I go anywhere, I need proof that Jed is alive," she said even though she knew her efforts to negotiate with the warden were futile.

"And I need proof that Rowe Cusack is dead."

Just as her attacker had, the warden was no longer bothering to hide the fact that he knew who and what Rowe really was. He wasn't afraid of the DEA. He had to be working with someone inside the administration.

She reminded him, "You saw the fax of that photo—"

"That photo is bullshit, Miss Kleyn," he interrupted, his voice rising in anger, "that fooled nobody."

"It would have worked," she insisted, "if you hadn't beaten Doc until he told you the truth."

He snorted again. "Did you really think a little girl like you could outsmart me?"

"Do you really think I'm stupid enough to come to

the prison alone without proof that my brother is still alive?"

"I don't expect you to come alone," he replied. "In fact I'd be quite upset if you did."

He wanted Rowe. Whoever had shot at them in the alley had definitely confirmed that the DEA agent had survived the warden's hit.

Tears stung her eyes as dread and panic clutched her heart. And if the warden had proof that Jed had disobeyed him, he would have already dealt with her brother.

"And I'd be quite angry if something had already happened to Jed and you were trying to lure me back to Blackwoods under false pretenses."

"Well, Miss Kleyn, I could take a picture for you…" he offered, "but we both know there's nothing like seeing someone in person."

The panic stealing her breath, she glanced toward the door, the locked door.

"I—I don't even know where I am right now." The abandoned airfield could have been anywhere. While she might not have lost consciousness from the glass, she had lost her focus for a while. She hadn't paid attention to how Rowe had driven to the airfield. "I'm not sure how soon I'll be able to make it to Blackwoods."

"You better make it soon, Miss Kleyn," he warned her. "Your brother doesn't have much time left. I'm about to commute his…*life*…sentences."

"Don't hurt him," she pleaded. "I'll get there." Somehow. Even if she had to burn down the hangar to get out.

But the sound of an engine drowned out the blower

on the wall unit, as a car approached. There was nothing on the abandoned airstrip but the hangar. Someone was definitely coming here.

To her. Or for her?

"Hurry back to Blackwoods," Warden James advised, "and bring that DEA agent with you or your brother will die." The line went dead.

Just like her brother probably already was. She knew that she would be a fool to fall for the warden's obvious trap.

But maybe the trap had already been sprung.

Maybe his plan had been to keep her on the phone until the cell was used to track down her whereabouts. She didn't know where she was, but she suspected the warden knew.

And he had sent someone to get her.

The door rattled as someone messed with the lock. The window into the hangar was too far from the door; she couldn't tell who was trying to get in, to get to her.

"Oh, God…"

She dropped the phone. It was too late to smash it beneath her foot or shove it into that burning pilot light to stop the call from being traced. She had already been tracked down.

But it wasn't too late to defend herself. She reached into her purse and pulled the scalpel out of her wallet. Then she rushed to the door just as it opened.

If this was the man from the alley, he was armed with a gun. And she had only the scalpel for a weapon. No matter that she was outarmed, she swung the blade, determined to not go down without a fight. Nobody was taking her alive.

Chapter Twelve

The warden breathed a sigh of relief and announced to his empty office, "We've got her."

And given the current situation, she was more important than Rowe Cusack. Macy Kleyn was the leverage he needed to regain control.

Shouts and shots continued to echo throughout the prison. And he suspected he smelled smoke. What the hell had they set afire?

How much more abuse could Blackwoods endure before the prison imploded? He glanced to Emily's picture. Instead of just straightening the frame, he needed to take down the entire picture and pack it away. He could keep Emily's picture safe. Maybe.

But he was more concerned about keeping Emily safe. From the truth…

Macy Kleyn would help him do that. She couldn't get to Blackwoods soon enough.

He pressed another button on the cell—for that one person's damn phone. Angry and impatient, he said, "I cleaned up your mess."

"It's over?"

"No. But it will be soon."

"I hope it's soon enough to protect the operation," his greedy partner declared.

Jefferson had once been that greedy. But right now the drug operation was the least of the warden's concerns. All he cared about was saving his ass. And the only way he could do that was to make sure Rowe Cusack was dead, along with everyone who had had any contact with him.

"I SHOULD HAVE KNOWN BETTER than to ever think you were defenseless," Rowe remarked as he ducked under the hand with which she swung the scalpel.

"Defenseless," she sputtered. "You were thinking that I'm defenseless?"

He grabbed her wrist and knocked the knife onto the floor. The metal clattered against the cement. "I knew you'd be pissed that I locked you in but this is ridiculous."

"I didn't think it was you at the door," she said. "I thought someone else was trying to get in."

And with the way she was trembling, he believed her. He wrapped his arms around her and drew her close. "It's okay. It's just me."

She was alone in the hangar. None of the agents had found her. Relieved that she was all right, he blew out a breath, stirring her hair.

But she wasn't all right. She shoved him back. "We need to get out of here. Now."

Surprised by the urgency in her voice, he narrowed his eyes and studied her face. "Did something happen? Was someone here?"

He hadn't noticed any tire tracks on the dirt lane

leading to the airfield, besides the ones from her car the night before and his truck when he had left before dawn.

She pointed a trembling finger toward the phone lying on the floor next to her purse. "He called me."

"Who?" She had taken that phone from a dead man's personal effects left in the morgue. How the hell had anyone realized she had it?

Maybe the dead man's relatives or someone else had reported it missing to the coroner. And her boss had given her up, proving again that no one in Blackwoods County could be trusted.

"The warden." She shook her head, her pretty mouth twisting with self-disgust. "I let him keep me on the phone, talking about Jed. He could have been tracing my location."

He grabbed up her purse and handed it to her. "We need to get the hell out of here. Now."

She picked up the scalpel from the floor and slid it back into her wallet. The leather had begun to fray from the sharp blade, and the vicious little weapon almost dropped out of it as she tucked the wallet into her purse.

"We need to go back to Blackwoods," she said, her voice steady with grim determination.

"That's the last place you're going." He shook his head. "It's too dangerous."

"It's too dangerous here, too," she reminded him. "The warden knows you're alive. He's not just guessing anymore."

He cursed. "So whoever shot at us in the alley is still in contact with the warden." This hadn't been a simple payoff for information. Whichever DEA agent had blown his cover hadn't done so for some quick cash. He or she had some type of arrangement with the warden. Perhaps they were even partners.

Tears shimmering in her eyes, Macy nodded. "Warden James threatened Jed. He said that if I don't go back and bring you with me he'll kill my brother. We have to go. Now."

Rowe sucked in a breath at how willing she was to sacrifice his life for Jed's. She'd easily made her choice. And just like when his parents had chosen drugs over him, he had come out last again.

The saddest part was that Jedidiah Kleyn was probably already dead. But Macy would know no peace unless she had done everything she could to save her brother. Rowe understood that. Even though he'd been just a kid, he had tried to save his parents, but the drugs had taken their lives despite his efforts. Of course he had been just a kid then. Now he was a man, so he ignored his own pain and disappointment.

He ignored the bed, too, the sheets tangled from their lovemaking, as he turned off the furnace and led her out the door.

"We'll take the truck," he said, holding open the passenger door. The car had no windows and the tire had gone flat from the crumpled fender rubbing against it. "It has a big engine. It'll get us there fast."

"He said to hurry." Fear darkened her brown eyes as she stared up at him, almost hopefully, as if she wanted him to assure her that her brother was all right.

He couldn't lie to her. "If the warden knows I'm alive, he knows where we are. He knows how long it will take us to get back to Blackwoods."

He shut the door on her, but it felt like more than glass and metal separated them now. It was as if last night had never happened, as if he had never been inside her—part of her. Had he dreamed it all?

He pulled out the disposable phone he'd purchased that morning. And, like the warden, he made some calls. He was going back to Blackwoods, but he wasn't going to walk blindly into the warden's trap.

Hell, no.

He was going to set a trap of his own....

WITH EACH MILE THAT THEY DREW CLOSER to Blackwoods, the muscles in Macy's already sore stomach tightened more, knotting with fear and dread.

"I'm going to drop you at a state police post," Rowe remarked, his voice nearly as cold and impersonal as the warden had sounded.

"What—why?"

"You're damn well not going back to the prison." Taking his gaze from the road, he spared her a glance. And his blue eyes were as icily cold as his deep voice.

What had happened to her lover? To the man who'd been so gentle and generous the night before?

She shivered. "I know. I know it's a trap. But if the warden got to someone in the DEA, don't you think he could have bought off the state police too?"

"Maybe the sheriff," Rowe said. "But I doubt he could buy off every law enforcement officer in the county. At least that's what I'm counting on."

"Is that who you called earlier?" He had made several calls while her stomach had clenched with nerves that someone would catch them at the hangar before they escaped. And her stupidity could have put them in danger.

"I called the DEA," he said.

She shivered at the coldness of his voice and his admission.

"But—but you know that someone at your agency betrayed you."

"And I have it narrowed down to three agents," he said, "so I called all three of them."

"But what if it's *all* three, working together?" she asked. Given the extent of the cover-up, she wouldn't be surprised if more than one agent was working against Rowe in the DEA. "Then you'll have no backup."

"I called in our group supervisor, too," Rowe said, "and the state police."

He had a plan, one he hadn't bothered to share with her. Instead they'd been driving in silence. She had been too scared to speak. But he just hadn't considered that she would want to know what he had planned to protect them. "I don't understand…"

"If I have any hope of saving your brother," he said, his words giving her the brief flash of the hope she hadn't dared to give herself regarding her brother's fate, "I can't storm Blackwoods alone."

"Rowe…" She blinked back tears, overwhelmed with emotion. They both knew it was too late for Jed. But that Rowe would lie to her…that he would risk his life to keep her hope alive…

Ever since he had returned to the safe house, there had been a distance between them that had felt far wider than the console between the truck's bucket seats.

She reached across now, clutching his arm, and tried to close that distance. "You can't go back there…"

"But that's what the warden demanded," he reminded her, his voice cold again.

And she realized that the distance between them was all her fault.

"That's what Warden James wants. It's not what I want." She had never intended to risk Rowe's life to save Jed's.

"But you wanted to go back to Blackwoods." His brow furrowed in confusion.

"He knows you're alive now. It's over. We both know it's over. Hell, even the warden knows it's over." But like her, the older man wasn't willing to go down without one hell of a fight.

Rowe tugged his arm free of her grasp and tightened his hands around the steering wheel. "I want to bring him in. I need him to tell me who gave me up."

"So you're bringing them all there together." She shook her head, which pounded with dread and fear. "It's too dangerous."

"There'll be too many witnesses for one of them to try something," he assured her. "I'll be fine."

"Then let me come along," she urged him.

"You can't be there when this goes down," Rowe said. "I need to leave you at this state police post." He started turning the wheel toward the freeway exit that led to the post.

She clutched his arm again. "No. You said yourself you don't know who you can trust. The warden wouldn't have been able to buy off everyone. But we have no idea who's working for him and who's not."

"I can't take you to the prison," he said, that muscle twitching beneath the heavy gold stubble on his jaw.

"So take me to the crematorium."

He shuddered. And she remembered he hadn't been any more comfortable there than he had been in the body bag, the morgue or the hearse.

"No one will look for me there," she pointed out. "So I'll be safer at the crematorium than my cabin or at the morgue."

"You think the coroner called the warden about the missing phone?" He had obviously already concluded that her former boss had betrayed her.

"Dr. Bernard had to have called someone about it," she said. "He reported it either to the warden. Or to the sheriff." Maybe he hadn't been paid off. Maybe he'd thought he was doing the right thing by reporting a theft to the sheriff, and the sheriff had given her up to the warden.

He cursed. "You're right. He could have called the sheriff. We can't trust anyone."

"Elliot's my friend," she said. "I can trust him." He was probably the only one in Blackwoods that she could trust—besides Rowe.

"He may not be there," Rowe warned her as he followed her directions to the narrow two-track that led to the back entrance of the crematorium. "Do you have the keys yet?"

She patted her purse in confirmation. "I'll be all right."

She doubted he would be the same, given that he was going back to the place where he had nearly been killed. Where he would have been killed if not for Jed helping instead of hurting him. What if Jed wasn't there to protect him again?

"I wish you wouldn't go," she said, "but I know that you have to do this." Just as Jed wanted whoever had framed him to pay for his crimes, Rowe wanted whoever had blown his cover and tried to kill him to be brought to justice.

"It's my job," he said, as if it was not personal at all. Maybe to him, given the icy way he was acting now, it wasn't.

He pulled the truck up to the back of the steel and post building but didn't cut the motor or even put the vehicle in Park.

"It's more than that," she insisted. "It's personal." And she wasn't talking about whoever had betrayed him but about the two of them.

He nodded. "My job is personal to me. I told you that my parents were drug addicts. That's why this job means so much to me."

"What about me?" she asked, wondering what she meant to him. Just a promise he'd kept to her brother? He was so much more to her than the man who kept saving her life. He was the man who'd given her a reason for living again. For loving...

"Macy..."

And she had her answer. He had consigned her to just part of his job, a promise he'd made to a man who'd helped him out.

While she wouldn't burden him with the words, she couldn't hold back the expression of her feelings for him. She leaned across the console again and wrapped both arms around his neck. And she pressed her mouth to his.

His lips stilled and his breath held, as if he tried to resist her. But then he groaned. His mouth opened, his tongue sliding across her lips, as he clutched a hand in her hair, holding her head close. He kissed her hungrily, with all the passion she remembered from the night before.

And when finally he pulled back, panting for breath as harshly as she did, his eyes weren't icy anymore. They gleamed with desire.

"Promise you'll come back for me," she asked, knowing that he was a man who took his promises seriously.

But instead, he asked one of her. "Promise me you'll stay out of the way?"

She opened the passenger door and stepped out into the empty lot. "It doesn't get any more out of the way than this."

He barely waited until she closed the door before he backed out, putting that distance between them again. This time physically as well as emotionally.

She should have told him her feelings. He deserved to know she loved him; maybe then he would have been as careful with his own safety as he'd been with hers. Her hands trembling, she barely managed to unlock the door. The wind had chilled as night began to fall, numbing her fingers so that she fumbled with the keys. Once she finally managed to unlock and open the door, she found that it wasn't much warmer inside the steel building than it was outside.

She considered starting a fire. But she didn't need

the smoking stack to draw any attention to her whereabouts. So instead she searched the small office for more clothes. Elliot usually kept a coat tossed over the back of his chair. As she lifted her friend's old parka, she noticed the picture on his desk. It was his band. She leaned over the chair to study the faces in the photo.

And now she realized why the man who had run her off the road and attacked her had looked vaguely familiar. She had seen him in this photo and probably playing guitar in Elliot's band when she'd gone to a couple of their gigs. But the dive bars were always so dark that she could barely recognize the guys she did know. And this photo was so small that she had to lean closer to make certain that she wasn't wrong.

The man had been Elliot's bandmate and friend.

The door rattled behind her, and this time she knew it wasn't Rowe. He wouldn't have had the key that slid in and unlocked the door. A gasp of surprise slipped through the man's lips as he noticed her standing inside the small office. He slammed the outside door shut and locked it behind himself.

She swallowed hard, choking on her nerves and fear. "H-hello...."

"Where is he?" Elliot asked, sparing her no greeting as he stalked toward her.

"The DEA agent?" She shrank back from the man she had been foolish enough to consider a friend. "He's on his way to the prison."

"Him and everyone else," Elliot remarked. "I'm talking about my friend." He gestured toward the picture on his desk that she'd been studying. "Where is *he?*"

She shrugged. "I don't know who you're talking about."

"Teddy." He pointed toward the bruise on her jaw. "I think he did that to you, probably when he ran you off the road yesterday. That was the last time I heard from him, when he called to tell me that he'd grabbed you."

"You told him to do that?"

Elliot shrugged, mocking her gesture of futile denial. Then he admitted, "The warden told me to do it. But I had already tried running you off the road once, the night before, when you left here with that damn drug agent in the back of the van."

"You saw him?"

He shook his head. "It wasn't what I saw. It was what I didn't see."

She furrowed her brow in confusion…until he pointed toward the ovens in the back room.

"No ashes, Mace," he said, then snapped his tongue against his teeth in a tsking noise. "You had taken the picture and started the fire. But you forgot the damn ashes."

How could she have been so stupid? So careless? "You called the warden."

"He'd already brought Dr. Bernard back to the morgue and found that the prisoner's body was missing," he explained. "Warden James and Dr. Bernard figured out it had come here."

"Why would you help the warden?" she asked. Her head pounded with confusion.

"Because I work for him," he replied matter-of-factly, as if she were an idiot for not knowing.

Maybe she *was* an idiot, because she still didn't understand. "You work here, for your dad."

He glanced around the small room, his eyes hard with hatred. It was evident that he dreaded this place nearly as much as Rowe did. "I have another side job besides the band, Macy."

She remembered his offering once to get her something to help her relax. She hadn't thought anything of it then, even as she'd refused him. "You're a drug dealer?"

"My dad pays me crap. Gigs don't pay much more than free drinks around here," he shared. "I need money—*real* money—to launch the band."

"You're talented," she praised him. And she wasn't lying. His band was good.

"Talent means nothing in the music business," he said with a snort of disgust over her ignorance and naïveté. "I need money."

Now she was lying when she said, "I can get you money, Elliot. I'll help you with your band." She'd thought she was helping him while she covered for him during his gigs. Maybe if she had done more, he wouldn't have become so desperate that he'd gone to work for the devil.

"I need my guitar player, too," Elliot said. "Where is he, Mace?" He stepped closer, and she noticed that same look in his dilated eyes. That same murderous intent that had been in his friend's gaze.

"Why would you turn on me?" she asked, her voice cracking with fear and emotion. "I thought we were friends."

"I wanted to be more than friends," he reminded her

of his earlier advances. "But you thought you were too good for me. Like you're so high-class when you got a brother rotting in prison for murder."

She flinched. Her pride wasn't stinging, though, but her heart was, over the image of Jed rotting anywhere. And Rowe joining him…

"Tell me what happened to Teddy," Elliot demanded, stepping closer to her. "Where is he?"

Because she wanted to hurt him, too, and because she needed to distract him, she replied, "Sitting in his SUV at the bottom of the ravine he nearly ran me into."

He staggered back a foot, shocked by her admission. "But how— He ran you off the road?"

She fumbled inside the purse clutched at her side, nicking her finger at the blade protruding from her wallet. "And I returned the favor."

"Is he dead?" he asked, his bloodshot eyes widening with horror.

She had always thought her young friend looked so rough because of the late hours he kept. Now she realized he wasn't just a dealer but a user, too.

"Is he dead?" he repeated his question, his voice rising to a shout of anger.

Fear gripped her at how out of control he was already becoming, but she nodded in reply to his question even though she risked more of his wrath. She couldn't let her fear paralyze her, or she would wind up as dead as Elliot's friend. Teddy.

"He's dead," she said.

Despite the cold in the unheated building, sweat beaded on the young man's face, trailing from his brow and dripping from his lip. "What—what the hell happened?" he stammered.

"I killed him," she replied matter-of-factly as she pulled the scalpel from her purse. "Just like I'm going to kill you."

But before she could brandish the weapon, he caught her wrist in a painfully tight grasp. "You're the one who's going to die today, Macy."

He was too strong, like his drugged-up friend, inhumanly strong. She couldn't pull free of him. She couldn't tug loose. She couldn't even drop the scalpel as his grip covered her fingers, pressing them into the sharp metal.

A cry of pain slipped through her lips. Elliot laughed, as if spurred on by her display of weakness. They had never truly been friends.

Like so many other people, he had always had his own agenda. He had been using her to cover for him with his dad.

"Elliot!" she screamed, hoping to get through to whatever decency the drugs hadn't stolen from him.

But he only laughed again, as if amused by her desperation and fear.

So then she kicked out, her foot connecting with his shins. The blow jammed her toes inside her shoe but didn't faze him at all.

He grunted and cussed, but he didn't loosen his grip. Instead he twisted her wrist, turning the blade toward her. Then he lifted her hand, despite her struggle, and directed it toward her neck. One nick of the scalpel into her carotid artery, and she would bleed out before Rowe could come back for her.

If he could come back for her...

He figured he had set a trap for the bad guys, but she suspected that he would be the one who got caught in that trap.

And Macy had figured Elliot was a friend, and she would be safe with him. Instead she had stepped into a trap of her own naïveté. She and Rowe might both die for their mistakes.

Chapter Thirteen

His instincts warned Rowe that something bad was about to happen. The muscles in his stomach were tightening. But with the trap he had set, it was inevitable that something bad was going to happen.

Or had already happened to Jed.

But Jed wasn't the Kleyn he was worried about. He kept glancing into his rearview mirror. The stack from the oven rose above the tin roof of the crematorium and even above some of the trees that surrounded the building. The lot wasn't empty now. The hearse had pulled in moments after Rowe had pulled out of the two-track onto the street.

The skinny guy inside hadn't even glanced at the truck. From the dent in his front bumper though, he didn't seem to be that careful a driver.

Rowe slammed on the brakes. The hearse was black, like the paint on the rear bumper of Macy's van. He'd thought that the SUV that had run Macy off the road had been the one that had tried the night before. But there had been no old dents on it before they'd sent it crashing down into the ravine.

"Son of a bitch…"

She thought the man was her friend. She would never

see it coming when he hurt her. Despite her resource-fulness and quick wits, she wouldn't be able to protect herself.

He jerked the wheel, spiraling the truck around in a tight U-turn. The front tire nearly dropped off the road into one of the deep ditches, but it caught the shoulder, spewing gravel behind it. Rubber squealed against as-phalt as he hit the accelerator and turned off the street to speed down the narrow two-track lane that led to the back entrance of the crematorium.

He parked behind the hearse, trapping it between his truck and the building. As he threw open his door, he reached for the gun he had taken off the last guy who'd tried to hurt Macy. And he hoped this kid wasn't armed, too.

With his free hand he grabbed the handle of the back door of the creepy metal building, but the knob wouldn't turn. The kid had locked it behind himself, locking Macy inside with him and help outside, so that she had no one to turn to—just as she had had nobody since her brother's incarceration.

Macy had learned to rely on and protect herself. But she didn't have to do that anymore. She had Rowe, even though he'd been too much of a pigheaded fool to make sure she knew how he felt about her.

The reinforced steel door wasn't keeping Rowe out. He shoved his shoulder against it and hammered his foot against it. But when he couldn't budge it with his shoulder or his foot, he jumped back into the truck. He rammed it into Reverse and then into Drive. Stomp-ing on the accelerator, he steered directly into the door.

He switched his foot to the brake, stopping short of

plowing right through the building, so that he wouldn't drive over Macy. He jumped out of the truck and scrambled around it to the door. But his bumper had only torn the wooden jamb loose. He still couldn't get through the door until he kicked it open far enough to squeeze inside. He did so with caution, keeping his head low in case someone fired at him.

They would have definitely heard him coming and had time to arm themselves.

But the room with the oven was empty. Of living people and dead bodies.

"Macy!" he shouted over the noise of the truck's idling engine. "Macy!"

Was he already too late? He passed through the oven room into a short hall.

Then he heard her cry. Soft sobs drifted through an open office door. His heart clutched with the fear and pain in her voice.

He rushed through the doorway into a scene of destruction. A desk and chair had toppled over, pictures and papers strewn across the room. He nearly missed Macy. The man was on top of her, his body covering hers as he trapped her to the ground.

What had the son of a bitch done to her? Had badly had he hurt her?

Rowe lifted his gun, training his barrel on the kid's back. But he couldn't shoot. As tightly as they were locked together, the bullet could pass through the man and right into Macy.

"Get off her!" he ordered, his shout echoing inside the metal building and hanging in the cold air like a puff of smoke. "Let her go!"

"Rowe!" she cried. And she shoved at the man until he rolled off her.

Blood smeared her face and saturated her shirt. Panic and fear stole Rowe's breath. He dropped to his knees beside her. "Where are you hurt?"

She shook her head.

He glanced at the man, to make sure he wasn't a threat any longer. The kid stared back at Rowe through eyes wide with shock and glazed with death. Blood covered him too, from the open wound in his chest.

The blood-covered scalpel clattered against the cement floor as it dropped from Macy's trembling hand. When was he going to accept that this woman could take care of herself? She didn't need him.

But then she threw her arms around his neck and clung to him, sobs racking her bruised and bloodied body. She had killed her attacker, but she hadn't come through their fight unscathed. Either physically or emotionally.

MACY HAD WANTED TO BE A DOCTOR to save people and yet she had just taken a life. That was a certain violation of the oath to do no harm. But she had never taken that oath.

"I—I killed him," she said.

"You had to," Rowe assured, one hand cupping the back of her head while his other one ran over her body as if he checked her for injuries. "You had no choice."

Elliot had landed a few blows. Enough to steal Macy's breath but not her strength. She hadn't lost her grip on the scalpel. But he'd lost his grip on her when she'd kicked him a lot higher than his shins.

He'd fallen back and doubled over in pain. But before she could get away, he'd recovered and come at her again. And when he'd charged her...

She had done what she'd had to in order to survive. "I—I thought he was my friend."

"I know..."

Of course he would understand her pain; he had been betrayed, too. She had given up med school and had moved to support Jed. But until now, she had never really understood how he'd felt. Someone had framed him; someone he'd known and trusted had betrayed him. Like Elliot had betrayed her...

"It was him that first night," she said. "He tried to run us off the road."

"I know," Rowe replied, his hands trembling slightly as they ran over her back, clutching her tightly against him. "I saw the hearse. It had a dent on the front bumper. It's why I came back."

"You're back," she said, pushing against his chest. Her shock easing, she was able to focus again. He was real; she hadn't conjured him up out of fear or because of some kind of psychotic break over being forced to kill to protect herself. "You shouldn't be back here. You should be at the prison."

With Jed. It was probably too late, but her brother deserved justice—for his death and for his false conviction. "Go."

He shook his head. "I'm not leaving you."

"You have to go," she insisted. "You put this whole thing in motion." To save her brother. "You need to be there to see it through, to see who gave you up to the warden."

He glanced down at Elliot's body. "I'm not leaving you here."

"He's dead." Because of her. But there had been no other way. He'd lunged at her when he'd heard the truck. He would have killed her if she hadn't killed him first. "He can't hurt me now."

"I'm still not leaving you alone," Rowe said as he helped her to her feet. "You're coming with me. I don't dare let you out of my sight again."

Relief shuddered through her. She didn't want to be apart from him either.

He leaned down and picked up the bloody scalpel, then wiped off the blade on the side of his jeans. "Even though you've proven again and again that you can protect yourself..."

She shook her head, never wanting to touch that sharp blade again. But he dropped it into her purse. Then he leaned down again and picked up the picture that had fallen to the floor during her fight with Elliot.

When she'd kicked him, he'd fallen back and knocked the chair over. Then when he'd lunged at her, he knocked her into the desk and sent it toppling over and the two of them onto the floor.

"This is the guy." The one he had killed to protect her.

"The warden told Elliot to grab me, but after he failed running us off the road, he sent his friend." Maybe he hadn't wanted to hurt her himself. But then she'd claimed to have killed his friend and he'd snapped.

Rowe sighed. "And both of them are dead and therefore unable to testify that the warden had given them their orders."

"I'm sorry...."

"It's okay," he said as he led her toward the broken-in door and the idling truck outside it. "We'll find other people to testify."

"You can testify," she said. "And Jed."

If he was alive...

"It's over, Warden," a deep voice taunted him through the bars of the cell in which they'd locked him, after storming his office and dragging him out into the prison.

But James refused to give in to the fear that niggled at him. These animals wanted to scare him. They wanted to make him suffer as they imagined he had made them suffer. But, despite their weapons, ones they'd stolen from guards they'd either hurt or killed, and their threats, he had nothing to fear.

They were too stupid to realize just how powerful he was. He had connections. He had bought off people in high places. He had backup—right outside the prison—that would save him and destroy all of them.

Beginning with Rowe Cusack and Macy Kleyn...

It was time. They would have made it from Detroit back to Blackwoods, because his partner already had. His partner was out there waiting for them.

"It's not over yet," he disagreed. "But it will be soon...."

That deep voice uttered a rusty-sounding chuckle. "You're so delusional that you think you're still in charge?"

"Delusional is your thinking I wouldn't have an insurance plan." He snorted in derision at their stupidity.

"Money won't get you out of this, James," the inmate advised. "Money doesn't mean anything in here."

No. Money wouldn't get him out of this situation. But despite his greed, he knew what was more powerful than money.

Love. It would get him out of Blackwoods and back with his daughter. And maybe she would love him enough to believe him despite what would surely be revealed about how he'd run Blackwoods.

"I know what matters," he assured his prisoners, who were now his jailers. He met the hard gaze of the man who ruled the rebels. "I know what matters most to *you*. And if you don't want me to destroy it, you'll do what I tell you."

The prisoner laughed again. "Let me guess…let you go?"

He nodded. The only way he could make certain that Macy Kleyn and Rowe Cusack were dead was if he killed them himself.

ROWE HADN'T NEEDED TO WORRY about reinforcements at the prison. The sheriff and the state police had barricaded the street leading to the entrance. If he hadn't grabbed his credentials off Jackson's body, he never would have been allowed past the blockade.

"You're Rowe Cusack?" the sheriff asked as he leaned down to the level of the open driver's window of the truck. The man was tall and young and mad as hell; his face flushed with anger, his voice gruff with it. "You're the one who called in everyone but me."

"I didn't know if I could trust you." He still didn't know, but he was pretty sure he couldn't. "Since I didn't call you in, why are you here?" He arched a brow and challenged the man with a direct question even though he didn't expect a truthful response. "Did the warden call you?"

"I came when the alarms went off," Sheriff Griffin York replied.

"What alarms?" Macy asked, leaning across Rowe to stare up at the sheriff.

"The alarms for the riot," he explained. "They report directly to my office."

"There's a riot?" Macy gasped.

"The whole place is on lockdown," the sheriff replied, leaning down farther to meet her gaze. He gasped himself when he noticed the blood on her clothes. "Are you all right, miss? Are you wounded?"

"She's fine," Rowe lied.

She was actually trembling with shock over her latest brush with death and with concern for her brother.

With a flash of pride, he added, "She just fought off an attacker."

"Attacker?" The sheriff's gaze trailed over her again, as if he could visually assess her injuries. "Who attacked you, miss?"

"Elliot Sutherland, a drug dealer," Rowe informed him. "*He* was on the warden's payroll."

"The kid from the funeral home?"

Macy nodded. He'd been more than that to her; she had considered the young fool a friend.

"What the hell's been going on in my county?" Sheriff Griffin York asked, his voice shaking with fury while his face flushed darker with wounded pride. "I didn't even know there was a DEA agent undercover in the prison."

"Nobody was supposed to know," Rowe replied. That was kind of the whole damn point of going undercover. "But somehow the warden found out."

York sighed, but it was ragged with his own frustration. "You keep blaming James for everything. Do you have any proof to support your allegations?"

"I came here undercover and left in a body bag," Rowe replied, and that should have damn well been proof enough that the warden was corrupt. Too bad the courts and apparently the sheriff would need more to press charges and convict. "Where is James?"

York jerked his head toward the prison. Despite evening falling, the place was ablaze with security lights and police flood lamps. "Inside."

"Have you had contact with him?" Because he wouldn't put it past the warden to use the riot as a diversion to slip out to a private airfield. The guy was probably halfway to someplace with no extradition treaty with the United States.

"We've had no contact with anyone inside," Sheriff York informed him. "We're waiting until the National Guard gets here and then we'll be storming the building."

Macy's breath shuddered out against the side of Rowe's face as she gasped again. "But won't that lead to a lot of casualties?"

"We don't know how many casualties there have already been," the sheriff replied, his jaw clenched and his dark eyes grim.

"But you know for certain there have been casualties?" Rowe prodded, with a silent plea for the guy to admit that he had no confirmation and would therefore continue to give Macy hope that her brother was still alive.

"We stopped a couple of guards as they were leaving," York admitted. "And held them for questioning."

That was good. Damn good that York had known to let no one get away. "And what were their answers?" he prodded.

"They confirmed casualties," he said.

Macy gasped again but this time it was a word. "Who?"

York shrugged broad shoulders. "We haven't been able to get inside yet, so we can't confirm anything."

"Who?" Macy repeated.

"According to the guards, the casualties were both inmates and prison staff," York replied. "But like I said, we won't know anything for certain until we can get inside."

"Whose decision was it to wait until the National Guard arrives?" Rowe asked.

"Yours," Sheriff York replied, his voice gruff with bitterness.

He shook his head in denial of the man's ridiculous accusation. "I didn't even know about the riot."

"It was the Drug Enforcement Administration's decision," York clarified. "One of the other DEA agents said we had to wait."

Until all the evidence and witnesses had been destroyed.

"Damn it!" He shoved open his driver's door. "Which agent? Which agent told you to wait?"

The sheriff stepped back as if to brace himself for an attack, and his hand settled on his holster. "The supervising special agent."

Dread tightened Rowe's stomach. The corruption had gone even higher than he'd feared. He slammed the door shut.

Through the open window, Macy stared at him, her brown eyes dark and tortured with fear for her brother. If Jed had been alive when the warden called her, he probably wasn't now. But Rowe didn't know that for certain, and he couldn't live with himself if his actions caused her brother's death and her pain.

"I'm going inside," he said.

"But your supervisor…" Sheriff York sputtered.

Rowe glanced around and saw none of his fellow agents. The state police and the sheriff's deputies had been pushed back here, away from the action, while the DEA SUVs were parked inside the gates.

"Someone blew my cover," Rowe pointed out. "Someone in *my* office."

"What does that have to do with Warden James?" York asked. Obviously he was as aware as everyone else was of how corrupt the prison warden was.

"Whoever betrayed me in the DEA is working with James." He lifted his shirt to show the bandage that Macy had put on his wound. "If this had gone any deeper, I'd be dead right now. If the inmate that the warden had ordered to kill me had really wanted to kill me…"

The sheriff sucked in a sharp breath. As if unable to

hold his opinion to himself any longer, he bitterly remarked, "The warden's a son of a bitch."

"And one of your biggest campaign contributors, if rumor is to be believed," Rowe said, gauging just how much this man could be trusted. He had to know before he made a judgment call that could affect everything. But could he trust his judgment?

Jackson hadn't betrayed him. Neither had Brennan. Maybe he could trust this lawman, too.

"That's not true." York shook his head in frustration. "He wants people to believe that, but I can show you my campaign records. I didn't take a damn dime of his dirty money. Where the hell do you think the DEA got the tip about Blackwoods—that something corrupt was going on there?"

While the tip had been anonymous, there had been enough information to warrant an investigation. Information that someone in law enforcement had likely compiled.

But that didn't mean that Sheriff York was that lawman. There was no time for the guy to prove his innocence, though. Rowe had to go with his gut. "You stay here. Don't let her out of your sight."

"Rowe!" Macy screamed, as if panicked over their separation. "What are you doing?"

Smoke rose from the prison. And the sound of rapid gunfire exploded like fireworks inside the concrete walls. She jumped out of the truck cab and grabbed at him.

"You can't go in there!" she protested.

"I can't *not* go in there," he said, his heart aching with the fear on her face.

"It's too late for Jed…." Tears streaked from her eyes, further smearing the blood on her face. "We both know that."

Rowe shook his head. "We don't know that. You Kleyns are fighters."

Jed had saved him once. Rowe had to at least try to return the favor.

"I'm fighting now," Macy said, clutching even more tightly to him. "I'm fighting for you."

"So am I." He pulled her hands from his arms and stepped back.

"I love you!" she said.

Her words swelled in his chest, filling his heart with an emotion he barely recognized. It had been so long since he'd loved or been loved. He couldn't say the words back yet.

So he turned away from her and headed toward the prison. Macy rushed after him, reaching for him again. The sheriff caught her, and held her back.

But it was as if Rowe took her with him; he could feel her, filling his heart. He glanced behind once, to where she struggled in the sheriff's grasp. Rowe loved her—that was why he couldn't break the promise he had made to her. He would get her brother out of prison. Even if it was the same way that Jed had gotten him out, in a body bag, he couldn't leave the man inside waiting for the National Guard that might never come.

Rowe walked through the open gates. But even though those gates stood open, panic pressed on his heart, as his old phobias rushed over him. He hated being confined. Hated small tight spaces. Most of all he hated Blackwoods Penitentiary.

The last time he'd left this hellhole of a prison he'd been zipped up in a body bag in the back of a coroner's van; he hoped he wouldn't be leaving the same way this time.

It wouldn't be the same, though. Because the next time someone zipped him inside a body bag, he'd have to be dead.

Chapter Fourteen

Macy struggled against the strong arms holding her back. "Let me go! Let me go!"

"He's gone," the man said, his deep voice rumbling in her ear.

Macy shivered and finally broke free of his steely hold. Maybe all her recent battles had drained her strength. Or maybe this man was just stronger than the other men with whom she'd had to fight for her life.

She whirled toward the sheriff. "What do you mean?"

For some reason Rowe had decided to trust the man. But she didn't. She *couldn't*.

"He's gone inside."

She glanced back toward the cement and barbed wire fence. She couldn't see beyond it except for the smoke that rose above it, blending into the darkening sky. "Why did you let him go?"

Because it was what the warden wanted. Without Jed or Rowe to testify against him, he wouldn't be charged with anything. This man certainly wouldn't arrest him unless a judge forced him to.

"Do you really think I could have stopped *him*?"

She suspected the sheriff wasn't just referring to the

fact that, as a federal agent, Rowe outranked him. He meant more that when Rowe was determined, nothing and no one could stop him. Her breath shuddered out in a ragged sigh of resignation.

"If *you* couldn't stop him," the sheriff continued, "I didn't stand a chance in hell of getting him to stay out here until the National Guard arrives."

"Sheriff York is right," a feminine voice murmured. "Rowe Cusack is a hard man to stop."

Macy shivered and it had nothing to do with the cold wind that spun the smoke rising from the prison into billowy clouds. She turned toward the red-haired woman who'd approached them. "Who are you?"

"DEA Special Agent Alice O'Neil," the woman replied, offering a smile that didn't quite reach her narrow eyes.

"Where's your supervising agent?" the sheriff asked her.

Alice shrugged. "I don't know exactly where he is now. The last time I saw him he was on the phone coordinating with the National Guard."

The sheriff gave a nod of satisfaction. "Good."

"They should be here soon," she assured the lawman.

It didn't matter to Macy. The Guard wouldn't arrive soon enough to save Rowe or her brother.

"Where did you see him last?" York repeated, determined to talk to the DEA agent in charge.

Alice gestured toward the fence. "Just inside there."

The sheriff started forward then glanced at Macy, as if just remembering his promise to Rowe to stay with her.

"Let him go," Alice coldly advised her. "Or you'll have more blood on your hands."

Macy shivered again but managed to nod at the sheriff's silent question, assuring him she was fine even though she was anything but. When the sheriff disappeared inside the fence, she turned toward the woman standing too close to her. The barrel of her gun dug deep into Macy's side.

"Why?" she asked.

"I would say that it's fairly obvious why." Alice laughed. "You're so young."

Lines creased the corners of Alice's eyes and the sides of her mouth, but she couldn't have been much more than forty. And with her pale skin and red hair, she was a beautiful woman. But her eyes were as cold as the warden's and nearly as empty as Elliot's. Except that Alice was alive and the man Macy had once considered a friend was dead.

"What does my age have to do with it?" Macy asked.

"You're young and idealistic, like Cusack. He still thinks he can save the world." She laughed again. "He can't even save himself."

"You blew his cover and gave him up for dead," Macy surmised. "But he survived."

The barrel jammed harder against Macy's side, this time in retaliation more than to simply subdue her. "Cusack only survived because of your damn brother."

Macy hated herself for the doubts she'd once entertained about her brother. He wouldn't have hurt the old prison doctor. He wouldn't hurt anyone. But had he been hurt?

The female agent seemed to think so because she

taunted Macy. "There won't be anyone inside who can help him now." Alice shoved Macy toward the truck. "Just like there's no one out here who can help you."

More gunfire emanated from inside the prison walls like the music from a rock concert overflowing stadium walls. But this was no concert with staged pyrotechnics. This was real. Flames burst through the roof with an explosion of gas and cement. All the police officers who had manned the perimeter rushed toward the prison now, right past Macy and the female DEA agent.

She could have called out, but they might not have even heard her over the noise from the prison. And if someone had heard her, she had no doubt that just as she'd threatened to shoot the sheriff, Alice would have shot anyone looking to save her, too.

Special Agent O'Neil opened the truck door and pushed Macy inside. "Keep going," she ordered, "over the console."

Macy went willingly to where she had dropped her purse. As she settled onto her seat, she reached inside the bag. "Where are you taking me?"

"Straight to hell," the woman murmured. She didn't reach for the keys that dangled from the ignition, though. Instead she stared through the windshield at the prison as flames rose from the roof.

Alice didn't even notice Macy digging inside her purse. When she finally fumbled the weapon free from her wallet, the sharp blade nicked her finger, and she sucked in a breath of pain and fear.

Rowe had wiped off Elliot's blood, but he hadn't sterilized it. But then, with this woman pointing a gun at her, catching a disease should have been the least of Macy's worries.

"I just killed a man I thought was a friend," she shared with the distracted agent. "Don't make the mistake of thinking I'm not capable of killing you, too."

"I'm not some stupid drug-dealing kid," Alice replied.

"You know about Elliot?"

"I know about everything. You think the warden was smart enough to handle this entire operation on his own?" She snorted her derision of his intelligence, just as James had earlier mocked Macy.

She suspected that their arrogance would prove the downfall for both of these criminals.

"Was?" Macy repeated. "Is he gone?"

"He's in there, too. Or whatever his prisoners left of him is in there…along with the body of your brother. And, in just a few minutes, your boyfriend will be torn apart." A smile of satisfaction crossed the woman's beautiful face.

"You're not a kid," Macy agreed, "but you're stupid to think that Rowe is going to die in there. He's more resourceful than you know."

And so was she.

HE COULD BARELY SEE THROUGH the smoke that hung heavy in the air. Alarms blared, reverberating inside his head along with gunshots and shouts and screams of pain. He'd thought Blackwoods was hell before; he'd had no idea what hell was…until now.

He had spent three weeks inside, but he recognized nothing of the open cells with cots burning inside.

Bleeding bodies were lying on the ground. He ducked down and rolled over people to check faces.

He had no equipment to address their injuries. Yet. The Guard and paramedics would treat them. Rowe had another mission entirely.

He was looking for one man.

But while he searched for Jed, someone searched for him. Heavily armed guards tried to take back the prison. But inmates had taken weapons from some of the fallen guards. Gunshots echoed off the walls, as bullets were exchanged.

He clutched his gun, but how effective was a nearly empty weapon against automatic rifles?

"There he is!" someone shouted.

He whirled just as a shot fired, striking the wall above his head. It wasn't a prisoner with a gun; it was a guard shooting at him. Rowe fired back, hitting the burly guard with the brush cut in the shoulder. The automatic rifle dropped, firing as it struck the ground. Bullets flew around the area.

Rowe hit the floor, rolling out of the way. He crept along the corridor, nearly on his belly, as another guard fired, covering his partner.

A prisoner, armed with one of the guard's guns, ducked through the open door of a cell and fired back. With a cry of agony the guard dropped to the ground.

But Rowe wasn't clear, for the prisoner caught sight of him and opened fire. Rowe lifted his gun and squeezed off his last shot. A bullet struck the prisoner's shoulder, driving him back inside the cell. Rowe lurched to his feet, ready to run. But before he could move, the inmate caught his breath and rushed forward, knocking Rowe to the ground.

He shoved the barrel of the rifle against Rowe's head, grinding the metal into his temple. "Now you're going to pay for that. You're going to pay for being a stinking narc—"

"Don't," a deep voice ordered as a shadow fell across Rowe.

"You wanna kill the Fed yourself?" the inmate with the gun asked, easing the barrel slightly away from Rowe's throbbing head.

"No," the big guy replied. "And you don't want to kill him either."

"But he's a Fed…"

"He's also the only person who can testify against the warden," the rational inmate said, pointing out Rowe's usefulness.

"We shoulda just killed James."

The big guy chuckled, a rusty rumble of sound that echoed like the gunfire or sounded like a hammer pounding nails into concrete. "Killing is too good for the warden. Too easy," he said with satisfaction. "He deserves to spend the rest of his life in hell. In *here*."

"Yeah!" the guy with the gun shouted his whole-hearted agreement.

The big guy sighed almost regretfully and said, "But that won't happen if you kill this Fed."

With a grunt of disgust and begrudging agreement, the armed inmate pulled the barrel away from Rowe's head. "All right, damn it. He can live to testify."

"Good."

"I hear a chopper!" The inmate ran off, the rifle

slung over his shoulder, as if he were eager to fire at the aircraft. If that chopper belonged to who Rowe suspected it did, the guy wouldn't get off a shot before guardsmen gunned him down as he very nearly had Rowe.

As he surely would have if this man, whose shadow Rowe lay beneath, had not intervened on his behalf.

A big hand reached down, lifting Rowe to his feet as if he weighed nothing. "How many times I gotta save your ass, Cusack?"

"You're alive!" Rowe gaped in shock that not only was Jedidiah Kleyn alive, but he looked relatively unharmed except for the bruises that Rowe himself had inflicted on him so that their struggle had looked real. But their efforts to make it look real had failed, as had their entire plan. "Macy's gonna be so relieved that you're okay!"

"I'm not relieved," Jed remarked. "What the hell are you doing back in here?"

"Looking for you."

"I told you I could take care of myself," Jed stubbornly reminded Rowe. "You needed to focus on Macy, on keeping her safe."

"Your sister's pretty good at taking care of herself, too." Must have been some family thing…self-reliance, pride and independence.

"Where is she?" Jed asked.

"Right outside," Rowe assured him, "with the sheriff."

Kleyn shook his head but then reached up to readjust the earpiece for the radio at his waist that he must have lifted from a guard. "That young sheriff's inside. He's looking for the warden."

"Is he dirty?" Had Rowe chosen the wrong time to trust his instincts? Had he chosen the wrong man to protect the woman he loved?

"I think he's looking for the warden because he wants to arrest him," Jed said, "not let him go."

"Where is the warden?" Rowe asked.

"The sheriff will find him."

"I should be the one to arrest him." To arrest the man who'd ordered his death and Macy's.

Jed shook his head. "You shouldn't be in here."

Rowe suspected the man didn't feel that way because he was concerned about his safety.

"You should be out there protecting my sister," he said, confirming Rowe's own feelings.

Rowe was about to deny that she needed protecting when that niggling sensation clenched the muscles in his stomach and that god-awful sense of foreboding washed over him.

"Come out with me," Rowe said. How happy would Macy be to see her brother alive and on the outside, even if he wouldn't be able to stay there until Rowe cleared him? "I'll protect you from the police and the National Guard." Bringing him out was a hell of a lot safer than leaving him in this hell....

Jed chuckled, as if amused by his concern. "I got this, Cusack. Get the hell out of here. That's what I intend to do."

"You're breaking out of prison?"

The big man didn't reply, just turned away from him as if he was already heading out of the maximum-security facility that had been his prison for the past three years.

"I can't let you do that," Rowe said. As a lawman, he couldn't stand idly by and watch a convicted killer— a *cop* killer—walk right out of the prison where he'd been sentenced for his crime.

He would stop Jed if he had to.

If he could…

How ironic would it be if the man he came back to hell to help was the man who finally carried out his order and killed him?

"THIS IS HIS GUN, you know," Alice remarked, staring down the barrel she had trained on Macy.

That had been one of Rowe's fears, that his mentor had been shot with his gun. "Did you kill Special Agent Jackson with it?"

Alice sighed. "That old fool didn't want the money. He wanted to pull Cusack out." She shook her head in disgust. "He didn't want the kid getting hurt."

"He was part of it?"

"No. He was like Cusack. Delusional. Even though he'd been on the job long enough to know better, he still thought he could make a difference in the world."

No wonder Rowe had respected and revered the man as much as he had.

"What little money he made on the job he donated half of to after-school programs." Alice snorted her disgust again.

"You don't think that you can make a difference in the fight against drugs?" Rowe did; it was why his job meant so much to him.

"I never thought that," Alice said.

Macy furrowed her brow in confusion. "Then why would you choose to work for the DEA?"

The redhead laughed. "It's where the money is, honey. The warden knew how to make money." And that was the kind of man Alice respected and revered—a killer. "Lots of it. Enough that as soon as I get rid of you, I can get out of here for good."

"You're going to shoot me, right here?" Macy challenged her.

Alice tapped the end of the barrel. "Silencer. Nobody will hear a thing, especially not over that racket."

The National Guard had arrived with helicopters and Humvees. The riot was over or would be soon. Alice wasn't going to wait any longer before she pulled the trigger.

So Macy lunged with the scalpel.

But the gun struck her. Not a bullet. Just the barrel against her arm, sending the scalpel flying across the dash…to the driver's side of the truck.

With the hand not holding the gun, Alice picked up the knife. "Maybe you should go out the same way your boyfriend just did."

"Elliot was not my boyfriend."

"I'm talking about Rowe. He committed suicide when he ran inside that prison to save a man who's already dead."

Macy ignored the flash of pain at the woman's matter-of-fact remark. She couldn't believe anything Agent O'Neil told her.

The redhead stared at Macy, her eyes narrowed in consideration of the lies she was about to concoct to cover her murder. "Maybe, overcome with grief over the loss of your boyfriend and your brother, you decide to kill yourself, too, rather than continue alone in the world."

"I would *never* kill myself."

"Trouble is that the only people who might know that about you are already dead. So…" Alice fingered the blade. "You know, if I were faking a suicide for anyone else, I would slit your wrists. But with your medical background, you would know that a person can survive slashing her wrists."

Damn. Macy had thought she was smart, but this woman was smarter. And she had done her research. She knew everything about her as well as everything about Jed.

Was she right about her fellow agent getting killed inside? Was she right that Jed was already dead?

Macy didn't know what beliefs to cling to anymore. This woman had confused and rattled her with her words more than the gun or scalpel she held. Or even with the murderous intensity of her stare.

"With your medical background, you'd know that the fastest and surest way to die is to cut your jugular." Alice had no more than made the declaration before she slashed the blade toward Macy's throat.

Chapter Fifteen

Warden James grimaced as he was handed into the back of the sheriff's cruiser. His arms stung, the handcuffs chafing his wrists. Some of the prisoners stood around, smiling even as National Guardsmen snapped handcuffs on them.

These men thought Jefferson James was no better than they were. Animals.

But he wasn't the only non-inmate in cuffs now. The guards who had survived the riot were being cuffed and placed into the backseats of state police cruisers.

Another man had been arrested as well, a man he had never seen before. The guy wore a suit and an attitude that suggested he'd been in charge of something.

But he wasn't the man who drew the warden's interest. He stared instead at the undercover DEA agent who stood next to the sheriff. If only Cusack had died...

"What the hell!" Rowe Cusack exclaimed as the sheriff patted down the pockets of the man that he had pushed up against the car. "I thought you were arresting the warden, not the special agent in charge of the DEA."

Sheriff York jerked his thumb toward the backseat.

"The warden's already been cuffed and read his rights. He's in there."

"Cusack, explain to this idiot that I am not in league with this corrupt official," the older man with the attitude ordered.

Warden James grinned over the incompetent sheriff arresting the wrong agent. His partner was still out there, still free. Despite the cuffs on his wrists, he wasn't without hope.

"You're the one who held off the raid on the prison until the National Guard got here," the sheriff explained to the agent he was cuffing, "giving your cohort time to destroy evidence."

James snorted. As if they thought he'd be stupid enough to leave evidence, or anything else incriminating, in the prison…

"It wasn't my idea," the snooty agent protested. "Special Agent Alice O'Neil urged me to wait."

The sheriff gasped. "Is she the redhead?"

"Yes," both Cusack and the other agent replied.

"I left your friend with her," York said. "I thought she'd be safe."

The warden leaned forward, just enough to catch the look of terror passing through the pale blue eyes of the DEA agent who should have been dead. "She would have been safer with me." James couldn't resist taunting them. "Because with Alice, there's no chance she's alive or that she didn't suffer greatly before that cold-blooded bitch killed her."

For a brief second, Cusack met his gaze. Behind the rage and hatred on the man's handsome face was fear and helplessness. Even though he wore no metal bracelets, he was cuffed almost as tightly as James was because he had just lost what mattered most to him—even more than his own life.

He had lost the woman he loved. James intimately knew the white-hot intensity of that unrelenting pain.

Now it was over.

EVEN ABOVE THE RACKET of the riot, Rowe heard her scream as he ran through the prison guards toward where he'd left Macy. He actually felt her scream, throbbing inside him, rushing through his veins with the adrenaline coursing through him.

While the warden had gloated, the sheriff had regretfully admitted to leaving Macy with Alice quite a while ago. They should have been gone. If Alice was as smart as he'd always believed she was, she would have forced Macy into his truck. She would have driven off with her, away from Blackwoods, away from Rowe.

But then, given the beating Jackson had taken before his death, Alice had toyed with him, too, just as she must have toyed with Macy. Why else would they still be close enough to the prison that Rowe could hear Macy's scream?

Killing wasn't just Alice's way of hiding her corruption; the woman must have actually enjoyed it. Why else would she have tortured a co-worker? First Jackson, beating him before she killed him, and now Macy.

So Rowe felt no compunction over pulling the trigger and sending a bullet straight into Alice O'Neil's twisted brain.

But had he fired it in time? Had she hit Macy with

that damn scalpel that she'd kept swinging at her as she taunted her with it?

He jerked open the truck door and pulled Macy from the passenger side. The dome light illuminated her pale face and wide eyes and the blood that already stained her clothes.

"Are you all right?" he asked, his voice shaking as badly as his hands as he lifted her in his arms. "Did she hurt you?"

"No…" But the denial slipped through her lips with a moan.

"You're not all right." She had been through hell because of him.

But instead of resenting him for it, she lifted trembling fingers to his face. "Are you all right?"

Rowe nodded in assurance. "I'm fine. Thanks again to your brother."

Hope brightened her eyes, chasing away some of the fear that haunted her. "He's alive?"

He couldn't tell her what had happened to Jed—not here, not with her being as fragile as she was.

"TELL ME WHAT HAPPENED to my brother!" Macy demanded. She had waited long enough, enduring the sheriff's questions and Rowe's pompous supervisor's questions. And any time she'd tried to ask about Jed, Rowe had silenced her with a look, as if she were supposed to deny the man who mattered most to her.

Or had mattered most…until she'd unzipped that body bag and found Rowe Cusack. She hadn't realized then what he would come to mean to her. She hadn't really realized it until he'd run into the middle of a prison riot.

Rowe lifted his gaze from the fire he'd started in her hearth while she'd taken the shower he'd insisted she have before they talked. It had felt good to wash off Elliot's blood, and Alice's....

She shuddered but refused to give in to shock again. She was stronger than that. She was Jed's sister. "Tell me..."

There had been casualties at the prison. It was all over the news, but he'd asked the sheriff, who'd driven them back to her cabin, to shut off the radio before Macy heard who those casualties were. Guards or inmates?

"Macy..." Rowe stared at her so strangely, his light blue eyes gleaming in the firelight, that he unnerved her.

Her breath caught in her throat, so that she could only whisper, "He's dead?"

"No, he saved my life." Rowe sighed wearily. "He saved my life twice."

She waited, knowing there was more to the story, more that Rowe struggled to admit to her. So, when he remained silent, she prodded him, "And?"

"So I let him go."

"What?" Shock struck her again, despite her best efforts to withstand it.

"There was a prison break."

"Several inmates escaped." She'd heard that on the news just as Rowe had had the sheriff shut it off. "Jed escaped?"

Before Rowe could reply, she shook her head. "But

he wouldn't do that. He'll never get his appeal, never be able to prove his innocence."

"He thinks it's the only way he can prove it," Rowe explained, "the only way that he can draw out the real killer."

"And you let him go?"

"He saved my life," Rowe repeated. "Twice."

"But all the authorities are going after the escaped convicts. They're considered armed and dangerous." Especially Jed, given that he had been convicted of killing a cop. "He could get killed."

"Your brother survived a riot and three years in a corrupt prison," he needlessly reminded her. "He's resourceful."

"He's innocent, though. Why couldn't he wait for you to prove that?" Dread clutched her heart. "He knows you don't believe him."

And if Rowe didn't believe in her brother, he didn't believe in her.

She'd declared her love, but he hadn't reciprocated. "Do you think he killed Doc, too?"

Rowe shook his head. "James had some guards kill Doc. It was what started the riot."

"But that was days ago."

"The warden had bypassed the alarm to the sheriff's office, thinking he could regain control. It wasn't until the prisoners got into the offices that he pulled the alarm."

"His arrogance will prove his downfall," she murmured.

"His pride," Rowe added. "His fear." And she wondered now if he were still talking about the warden. He closed the distance between them and caught Macy's hands in his, tugging her toward the bed as she had tugged him just the night before.

She dragged her feet, going but not quite willingly, not until she knew for sure what was really going through his head. "Rowe…?"

"I know your brother didn't kill Doc," he replied, "and I know he didn't kill anybody else either."

"You believe in him?"

"I believe in *you*," he said. "And you believe in him."

"But do *you*?"

"Your brother is a hero, not a killer," he said, as if he believed it. He wasn't just humoring her; he respected her brother as much as she always had. "We'll prove his innocence."

"We?"

"I need you, Macy, by my side…for the rest of our lives."

"What are you saying?"

"That I love you." He lowered his head and brushed his lips across hers. Then he reached for the towel she had wrapped around herself and pulled it loose until it dropped to the floor. A ragged breath slipped through his lips. "You're so beautiful…."

She skimmed her fingers across his tautly clenched jaw. "You're not so bad yourself…"

He grinned, and warmth spread through her, his happiness warming her more than the fire. "Will you marry me?"

She laughed and reminded him, "We've only known each other a few days."

Before, when she'd had her life all mapped out, she

had planned when she would get officially engaged: after she'd graduated premed. And when she would get married: after medical school but before she started her residency. And when she would have children: after she'd gone into private practice. But nothing in her life had gone according to her plans.

If it had, she never would have met Rowe Cusack, and that would have been far more tragic than her de-railed plans.

"Does it make a difference how long we've known each other?" he asked, stepping back.

But he didn't seem mad about her reaction to his proposal, because he pulled off his shirt and tossed it down onto her towel. Then he undid his belt and, with a pop of a snap and a rasp of a zipper, he dropped his jeans and his boxers.

Her breath escaped in a sudden rush.

"Do you think you'll love me less when you get to know me more?" he prodded her, as if he believed time was the only reason she hesitated.

She shook her head, sending droplets from her wet hair flying. Some landed on his chest and trickled down over the sculpted muscles. She leaned forward, flicking out her tongue to lick them away.

His flat nipples puckered. She closed her lips over one and tugged then flicked her tongue across it. He clutched his hands in her hair and tilted her head up. Then his mouth covered hers, kissing her deeply.

When he finally pulled back, she panted for breath. "I don't think I can love you more," he said. "But then every time I look at you, it's like my heart stretches, making more room for you."

"Rowe..." Tears stung her eyes.

He lifted her onto the bed and followed her down, covering her naked body with his. Skin slid over skin and lips over lips. They loved each other with their mouths and their hands, kissing and caressing.

Her need for him built until she ached with wanting him. Then he parted her legs and joined their bodies, thrusting deep inside her, filling the emptiness she hadn't even realized she'd felt until she'd met him. They found their rhythm together, her rising to meet his every thrust. She clutched his shoulders and his back and locked her legs tight around his lean waist. She would never let him go.

But then the passion exploded, curling her toes and pulling a scream from her lips. He buried himself deep and, with a shout of release, filled her with his pleasure. Then he clasped her tight against his madly pounding heart, holding her close.

And she knew it didn't matter how long they'd known each other. The only plans that mattered to her now were the ones they would make together.

"I will marry you," she said, pressing a kiss to his lips.

"When?" he asked. "I don't want a long engagement."

"Then we better get busy," she said. "Because I can't get married until we find Jed, so he can give me away."

Rowe stared down at Macy's face, her cheek pressed against his chest as she slept in his arms. He wanted to slide a gold band on her finger now, to make her his wife before she changed her mind.

Because he couldn't have gotten this lucky. The most amazing woman in the world couldn't have fallen for him. He didn't doubt her love now. But would it last if he couldn't keep his promise to her?

"It doesn't matter, you know," she murmured sleepily. "Even if you can't help my brother, I will never stop loving you."

He grinned. Even asleep, she knew what he was thinking. Her quick mind never shut off.

"I will never love you any less," she vowed. "Only more. More and more every minute of every hour of every day of the rest of our lives."

Maybe she wouldn't love him less if something happened to Jed. But she wouldn't be truly happy, completely happy, until her brother was safe and exonerated.

"It matters to me," Rowe said. "I promise you that I will save your brother."

He owed the man. Jedidiah Kleyn hadn't just saved Rowe's life—he had given him a life when he'd sent Rowe to Macy.

In a body bag.

Now Rowe hoped he could keep the promise he'd made to his fiancée…because he suspected the person from whom Jedidiah Kleyn most needed saving was himself.

HE WAS ON THE WRONG SIDE of the bars again. But this time animals hadn't locked him up. Men of law and order had—arrogant, self-righteous men who would not accept bribes.

Yet.

Jefferson James had found few men that he had not been able to buy. But if he had not been able to buy them off, he had been able to kill them. Until Rowe Cusack.

Hell, he hadn't even been able to kill the girl. No one had.

Jefferson's partner was dead. His guards were either dead, too, or locked up like he was. While Jefferson could find someone else willing to try to kill Cusack and the girl, he doubted they would be any more successful than the others had been. According to his lawyer, their testimony wouldn't be the problem anyway. It was all hearsay or inadmissible.

There was only one person about whose testimony Jefferson needed to worry: Jedidiah Kleyn. Right now every law enforcement officer in the area was out looking for the escaped convict. Other inmates had gotten out during the riot, but it was Kleyn that everyone sought because of what he was. A cop killer.

Jefferson had to make sure that they didn't bring him in alive. Even behind bars he had power and influence—enough to put out a shoot-on-sight order on Kleyn. He needed the man dead. Very dead.

JED KLEYN STOOD IN THE SHADOWS of the dark woods surrounding the burning prison. He was no longer inside those cement walls and barbed wire. No longer locked behind bars like an animal.

But he wasn't free. He wouldn't be free until he finally proved his innocence. Three years had changed him. It had taught him things about survival that he hadn't even learned during his tours of duty in Afghanistan. Now he fully accepted that in order to prove he wasn't a killer, he might have to become one.

* * * * *

SUSPENSE

Harlequin®

INTRIGUE®

COMING NEXT MONTH
AVAILABLE APRIL 10, 2012

#1341 SON OF A GUN
Big "D" Dads
Joanna Wayne

#1342 SECRET HIDEOUT
Cooper Security
Paula Graves

#1343 MIDWIFE COVER
Cassie Miles

#1344 BABY BREAKOUT
Outlaws
Lisa Childs

#1345 PUREBRED
The McKenna Legacy
Patricia Rosemoor

#1346 RAVEN'S COVE
Jenna Ryan

Harlequin

ROMANTIC
SUSPENSE

Danger is hot on their heels!

Catch the thrill with author

LINDA CONRAD

Chance, Texas

Sam Chance, a U.S. marshal in the Witness Security
Service, is sworn to protect Grace Brown and her
one-year-old son after Grace testifies against an infamous
drug lord and he swears revenge. With Grace on the edge of
fleeing, Sam knows there is only one safe place he can take
her—home. But when the danger draws near, it's not just
Sam's life on the line but his heart, too.

Watch out for

Texas Baby Sanctuary
Available April 2012

Texas Manhunt
Available May 2012

www.Harlequin.com

HRS27772

Taft Bowman knew he'd ruined any chance he'd had for happiness with Laura Pendleton when he drove her away years ago…and into the arms of another man, thousands of miles away. Now she was back, a widow with two small children…and despite himself, he was starting to believe in second chances.

Harlequin Special® Edition® presents a new installment in USA TODAY *bestselling author RaeAnne Thayne's miniseries,* THE COWBOYS OF COLD CREEK.

Enjoy a sneak peek of A COLD CREEK REUNION

Available April 2012 from Harlequin® Special Edition®

A younger woman stood there, and from this distance he had only a strange impression, as though she was somehow standing on an island of calm amid the chaos of the scene, the flashing lights of the emergency vehicles, shouts between his crew members, the excited buzz of the crowd.

And then the woman turned and he just about tripped over a snaking fire hose somebody shouldn't have left there.

Laura.

He froze, and for the first time in fifteen years as a firefighter, he forgot about the incident, his mission, just what the hell he was doing here.

Laura.

Ten years. He hadn't seen her in all that time, since the week before their wedding when she had given him back his ring and left town. Not just town. She had left the whole damn country, as if she couldn't run far enough to get away from him.

Some part of him desperately wanted to think he had made some kind of mistake. It couldn't be her. That was just some other slender woman with a long sweep of honey-blond hair and big, blue, unforgettable eyes. But no. It was definitely Laura. Sweet and lovely.

Not his.

He was going to have to go over there and talk to her. He didn't want to. He wanted to stand there and pretend he hadn't seen her. But he was the fire chief. He couldn't hide out just because he had a painful history with the daughter of the property owner.

Sometimes he hated his job.

Will Taft and Laura be able to make the years recede…or is the gulf between them too broad to ever cross?

Find out in
A COLD CREEK REUNION
Available April 2012 from Harlequin® Special Edition®
wherever books are sold.

Celebrate the 30th anniversary
of Harlequin® Special Edition® with a bonus story
included in each Special Edition® book in April!

Harlequin Blaze™
red-hot reads

**Sizzling fairy tales
to make every fantasy come true!**

Fan-favorite authors
Tori Carrington and Kate Hoffmann
bring readers

Blazing Bedtime Stories, Volume VI

MAID FOR HIM...

Successful businessman Kieran Morrison doesn't dare hope for
a big catch when he goes fishing. But when he wakes up one
night to find a beautiful woman seemingly unconscious on the
deck of his sailboat, he lands one bigger than he could ever
have imagined by way of mermaid Daphne Moore.
But is she real? Or just a fantasy?

OFF THE BEATEN PATH

Greta Adler and Alex Hansen have been friends for seven years.
So when Greta agrees to accompany Alex at a mountain retreat
owned by a client, she doesn't realize that Alex has a different
path he wants their relationshiop to take.
But will Greta follow his lead?

Available April 2012 wherever books are sold.

www.Harlequin.com

HB79679